Short Story Collection

Maiden Voyage-A Lighthouse Tale

Kiss Ride

String the Cranberries

Books by Kim Troike

KISS RIDE
Into the Vines

&

Books by Caroline Clemens

Maiden Voyage-A Lighthouse Tale

String the Cranberries

Brie's Story

Someday

The Pilot Log,

Autumn Quotes, Chocolate for Lilly

Three King Mackerel and a Mahi Mahi

Kiss Ride by Kim Troike
Copyright © 2019 by Kim Troike

For information about special discounts available for bulk purchases, sales promotions, fund- raising and educational needs, contact:

@clemensnovels
https://carolineclemens.com/
ISBN 978-1-988680-07-1
ISBN 978-1-988680-06-4
Edit and Copy by S. Jeyran Main
C. Hendi cover artist from SelfPubCovers

These novels are a work of fiction. Names, places, businesses, events, buildings, people, and circumstances are either used fictitiously, or are the author's imagination to build creatively.

Table of Content

String the Cranberries

Maiden Voyage

A Lighthouse Tale

By Caroline Clemens

Chapter One

GONE FOR A WEEK

Kyle had been gone for a week living at the Marblehead Lighthouse. His research for a Master's Thesis was important and he had received special privileges to actually inhabit the place. In particular, he told me not to visit, that we would once again be together on Christmas Day. We had parted with harsh words and this bothered me to no end. How did he feel? I had so much to say to him. We had been dating for just a little over a year. How could one week be so cruel to me and the week before Christmas no less? I needed an angel's mercy.

I decided to walk to town and not attend a neighbor's party where my family gathered. Mother understood. Her last words were, "Don't go to the lighthouse, you know what he said."

"I know mom, I'll just take a good long look on my way to the Maiden Voyage." Oh Mother, just leave me alone, I thought. Everyone please leave me alone. It's Christmas and I'm in love, and I miss my dear Kyle. There I said it.

"Oh, Bridgette. That's fine, enjoy your time. I saw on the television it may snow heavily after nine o'clock."

"Perfect. Just in time for Christmas!" That sounded more excited than I actually was at this moment. "See ya later, mom." I opened the front door and closed it quickly behind me. This rattled mother's garland around the front door. She had placed red velvet ribbon that adorned the corners. It made me notice that our house needed a solid coat of paint. Since Dad died things didn't quite get done as fast. Poor Mother, she had her hands full with my brothers and sisters. Enough of that now. After all, Christmas was about our wishes and dreams. We were allowed to be a bit selfish after we made, bought and wrapped gifts for others. The surprise was always so much fun.

I stepped down the three old wooden steps onto the light dusting of snow that we had received yesterday afternoon. I was twenty-two years of age and my boyfriend just turned twenty three December 10th. We were in love like the mutual thing everyone talks about. I was sure the day I met him and pretty certain he thought the same way. What cruel twist of fate was this though? Hold on, one more day. Tomorrow was Christmas.

I had decorated the tree out front for mother, and for my brothers and sisters, who were quite younger than myself. For some reason since I'd gone to college, they all seemed more capable than when I left them a few years back. I remember the look on my mother's face when she dropped me off as she piled the kids back in the car, all four of them. Thankfully, she never moved away and had family nearby, which helped her out. I never looked back. I was smart enough to know this was my lucky break. Do good in college and the world would be mine.

So why was I at home doing nothing? I was waiting on my honey to finish his college. He will finish in March and then who knows? We hadn't talked about what to do as yet. But I felt good about us and I know he did too.

Things were quiet, and quite white. Dusk would soon be setting in to offer me a peaceful setting. The bar I was headed to, Maiden Voyage, was about a mile and a half away, not far at all, and of course, I would pass the lighthouse on the way. If Kyle was outside, I'd wave, if not he wouldn't see me as the window faced the lake. I began to think about how bored he must be. That's precisely what he wanted to record down on paper, his thoughts, loneliness, and the possible magnitude of the position held by others so many years ago. What could possibly be similar in today's standards? My mind wondered as I walked the street's edge, near the grass line, covered in snow.

The trees were barren and winter had set in out here on Marblehead. Smoke came out of chimneys and floated free away from the homes. My friends would be coming out here tonight after their dinners at friends or family. It was our hangout away from home, a home away as they say. Johnny, the bartender, I'm sure would be there. He entertained us every time we went. The Maiden Voyage was a classy joint with wooden features and brassy nautical accents. One felt like they walked into the 1st class section on an old ship. We were lucky to have such a nice place in our small hometown. Where would I go someday if I moved away? Possibilities seemed endless.

I began to think about my Kyle who was tall and broad shouldered with brown wavy hair and brown eyes, which seemed to only look at me. He made me feel divine. I missed him. Tomorrow.

Right around the bend I decided I would walk very slowly and look over at the lighthouse. I persisted onward. I took a deep breath and tried to smell the air, only to choke up a little when I saw the lighthouse standing there. I crossed the street and walked just a little upon the parking lot, getting a little closer. I looked around for Kyle but no one was lurking anywhere. He'd told me if we used a cell phone the whole project would be nullified. He had to act like it was 1850. Imagine that.

I shook my head in despair. Of course, I walked tonight to maybe get a glimpse, else I'd have just driven. I felt ridiculous. Nevertheless, I loved him and what I wouldn't do I don't know. Goodness.

My mother, a hairdresser, had fixed my hair earlier in the day. She called it a basket of thanks loaded with braids and gentle twirls. She even interlocked a strand of pearls throughout. My mother was drop dead gorgeous and we told her this quite often. A kindhearted soul, we all wanted her to get married again to see the light turned back on. When we told her this she smiled, and said, "It will happen when it will."

I wasn't wearing a Christmas sweater tonight. No. No. Somehow tonight called for a dress with boots of brown leather and a special necklace my father gave to me years ago. I felt complete, except of course, where was he? Oh yeah, in the lighthouse. I couldn't take it anymore. I was going mad. I needed to see my friends.

I picked up the pace and smiled. I hoped Kyle got an A on his thesis and graduated in March. I wondered if he'd find anything in particular that no one else knew. Knowledge, sometimes it crept up and seemed foreboding, like no one ever knew that before. My degree was in Fashion Design, pragmatic to the core. I wanted simplicity and everyone to care more about themselves. A life well-lived is the best and this is how my mother coped with my father's death. He lived it well, so we should too.

I glanced over at the beautiful red barn. It looked even prettier surrounded by the white snow. The roof had a partial dusting as did the limbs on the trees nearby. I'd almost say winter is mighty pretty, certainly though, not the prettiest sight around these parts. Summer held that reserved spot all to herself.

Before I knew it the Maiden Voyage was before me. I turned back ever so slow for one more look. I knew what I would do, break the rules, but only on the last night. I would go and see him closer to midnight. He couldn't turn me away. I was sure of it. I quickened my pace, happy now, as I had a plan.

The parking lot was half empty, half full, depending on how you viewed Christmas Eve. I always loved Christmas, so quiet, so full of wonderment, so white when blessed by snow like tonight.

Did I mention my boyfriend was a weightlifter? Well, not the professional kind but hey muscles were muscles and he had them. Yup, a real friendly social kind of guy, so this was probably killing him more than me. I walked through the door and headed for the bar.

Things were quiet with a few families and a couple of the regulars. I went and sat next to my friend Brittany and her beau Michael. She had a very old lady sitting with her.

Chapter Two

THE MAIDEN VOYAGE

"Hello dear!"

"Hello and Merry Christmas Johnny!"

"Merry Christmas! What will you have? It's on the house."

"What should I have?"

"A Christmas Ale fresh from Cleveland," he said.

"Sounds great." I concluded. "Hello Brittany! Merry Christmas to you and Michael. Who's your friend?'

"Merry Christmas, Bridgette," said Brittany. Michael smiled. "This is my great-great grandmother, Mary Patterson. But you can call her May!"

I focused on May and her dazzling smile. She had makeup on and was drinking a glass of chardonnay. No way. Man, I hope to be just like her someday ... a hundred years old taking it all in sitting at her great-grandsons bar. Ha. "Merry Christmas May! Nice to meet you."

"Merry Christmas," she replied. She took my hand and held it for a moment. Then she patted it with my hand in the middle of hers but said nothing. Oh well.

"How come I never met you before?" I asked.

She replied. "I've been down south for the winters, first time up in a

7

while."

"I must have missed you during the summertime."

"That's when I travel." She smiled.

"Here ya go." Johnny handed me the Christmas Ale. I took a swig and looked around at all the decorations inside. He had a medium size Christmas tree near the front window, full of lights and red bulbs, a garland of cranberries and even a popcorn string. Near the back of the bar was a train that ran around the upper area of the wall close to the ceiling. It looked like it had been handed down from a couple generations or so.

I sat down next to Brittany and her relative named Mary or May as she liked to be called. I was already being distracted from my temporary insanity and that was a good thing.

"You going to be here for a while?" asked Michael.

"Yes. Whenever Johnny closes, I'll leave. Nothing really happening for me tonight with Kyle at the lighthouse and Mom taking the kids to church and then tucking them in while they dream of Santa and his sleigh."

"What? You want to miss that?" asked Bridgette.

"I was there every year for all of it since they were born. Mom is giving me the night off. She even fixed my hair. Do you like?"

"I keep telling your mom she needs to open a shop. She's very good," said Johnny.

"I agree. She said next spring. Everyone will be in school and she'll get a job."

"I'll be her first client. Sign me up," said Brittany. "What should I have her do?"

"Highlights. You need highlights on that dirty blonde hair, something that will make someone take a second look." I winked at her knowingly as I wanted to get a rise from Michael.

"Wait a minute, no second looks," said Michael. He put his head in his hands, then looked up and laughed. "I'm headed home. I can't take any more of this girl talk. Out of here."

"Okay baby, see you later at your house," said Brittany.

"What time are they getting your Grandma May?" asked Michael before he departed.

"In about an hour or so," replied Brittany. Brittany looked very pretty tonight, she wore a burgundy velvet top that willowed over her lower figure, which had off white leggings and light tan leather boots. I guess we were all dressed up, more than usual, on this most special of eves, Christmas Eve. My own dress of burgundy-dark green plaid was laced over with black stitching and fully buttoned down the front. My brown leather boots kept me warm and slightly taller than norm.

"What did you get him for Christmas, anything special?" I inquired.

"Of course, I had to get something special. I bought him a watch and a new fishing pole."

"Wow. You went all out."

"Fishermen don't usually sport a watch but in this case, I wanted him to have one so he would know how long he is out doing his hobby on the water." Both of us laughed out loud.

"Good deal. Now he'll know, even if he loses power on his phone, what time it is."

Johnny had a few TV's on and one was showing "What a Wonderful Life." Another had the news on with all the late shoppers scrambling around in traffic after purchases made in malls across America. And yet another had some church scene with filled pews and a chorus singing with an instrumental band near the pulpit. I gazed at the church and thought about getting married in a church like that someday. Didn't one have to actually belong to a church to get married in such a venue? I wondered. I decided right then I wanted a big church wedding.

Church must have let out because a couple of groups meandered in and began playing the jukebox. There was no band tonight just Christmas tunes to warm our hearts and maybe join in unison with friends for a lyric or two or three.

Brittany and I ordered a perch sandwich with fries, vinegar and tartar on the side. One of my favorite songs came on and I couldn't help but belt out a line from Feliz Navidad. I ordered another Christmas Ale and waited for my favorite sandwich of all. I believe I could eat one of these every day. What if they didn't have these wherever I moved to? Come to think of it they probably wouldn't so I'd have to find a new favorite.

A couple of the guys playing pool began to get loud enough that we all looked over. Johnny called over to them, "No fighting guys. It's Christmas Eve."

One of the regulars walked over near the table. He just had to stand there because his presence could not be denied. Both of them looked at him and quickly resolved their dispute.

"Johnny, you really should pay him a bouncer fee. What he does for your place, by keeping the peace throughout the year, is undeniably a good thing."

Johnny winked at me. "I do."

"No way, seriously?"

"No wonder," said Brittany.

Johnny looked out the front window. "Looks like the lake just kicked it up a notch."

We followed his gaze and agreed with him.

Brittany and I enjoyed our food and talked about old times for a while. We'd grown up together and I left for college while she never did. She was happy she said. She liked her life and her man. They'd been planning their future life together, house and babies, etc. I told her about my present situation and did not know what the future held. I was kind of stalled at the moment. I wasn't worried just didn't know my future.

"My future is right here, you are looking at it. We'll see, maybe next year things will get moving. After he turns in his thesis and after he graduates, then I'll let you know."

May must have heard us talking about the lighthouse and my uncertainty of plans because she called Johnny over. "Johnny, get that old journal out from upstairs."

Johnny retreated and went up the back staircase to the second floor. I looked at May but she gave nothing away. I turned my gaze to the front window again and it looked like a winter storm coming on fast. Nothing unusual really. Just that I better keep tabs on it so I could make the trek home without losing my way.

The front door opened briskly with a heap of cold air and in walked the family member for May. She got up from her bar stool and stood before me. "Bridgette, tell Johnny you can borrow the old journal for a day or two then return it back to him."

"An old journal?"

"Yes, dear. I think you'll find it just what you need tonight."

I looked at her and didn't know what to say.

"Take it with you when you visit the lighthouse on your way home," she whispered to me so no one else would hear.

"Thank you, I guess."

"Merry Christmas!" She left.

"Merry Christmas to you too!"

Chapter Three

JOHNNY HANDS ME THE JOURNAL

hen he returned his great-great grandmother May had left. He looked around with the journal in his hand. Then he set it down next to the cash register like he would not let it out of his site.

Around nine-thirty Brittany said goodnight and asked if I needed a ride. I said I didn't.

I waved goodbye with wishes for a Merry Christmas and promised I'd see her for New Year's Eve. She said likewise.

"Bridgette, do you want anything from the menu before I send the cook home tonight?"

"You know I will order something to-go. I'll have the same as I ate earlier."

"Sounds good."

"What time are you closing?"

"Probably in an hour or so, after this church crowd leaves, that is the ones that came from early church and the ones that have yet to go for the midnight mass."

"I'll leave then too."

Johnny looked out the window, it was dark and one could see the swirls of snow going this way and that. "Maybe I should give you a ride."

"I tell you what, I'll leave before you, that way you'll see me almost home or at least near the lighthouse on the way."

"Perfect."

"May said to let me borrow the old journal for a couple days, then to return it to you."

Johnny looked right at me, seriously contemplating what I had just said.

"Did she?"

"Yes, she did."

"May, she doesn't do things like that you know. She protects all her old things upstairs. No one touches them, so I was surprised she asked for it."

"Well if you don't want to that's okay," I said more perplexed now that it seemed an important item.

"Let me put your order in," Johnny said and went to the kitchen.

I looked around and people were enjoying themselves talking, laughing, and some were singing. One more day. At least I had taken up some time. Now I was getting eager for the rest of Christmas Eve.

Johnny was gone for a very long time. I sat there dreaming a little and wondering if all my brothers and sisters were going to be surprised tomorrow morning. Mom did a nice thing for me tonight. I was much older than all of them, and she let me be a young grown up in-love I might add. She may have remembered just what that was like. After all, she was young once and fell in love with my Dad. I'd help her tomorrow morning amidst the chaos and strewn paper everywhere. I was helping with dinner and the relatives coming to see us. With any luck Kyle would make it for dinner too. I was hopeful, anyway.

"Here you go and I know where you're headed. Going to feed someone holed up all week?"

"Yes. What time is it?"

"Eleven fifteen."

"Okay, I'm leaving. Let me pay up."

Johnny packed up my order with a six pack of Christmas Ale. He turned and looked my way and then back to the old journal. "If May said for you to take this then I'll trust you. Please return it in a couple days. Merry Christmas!"

He handed me the journal after he put it in a plastic bag with extra paper around it.

"Merry Christmas Johnny! Thank you!" I smiled at him and hurried for the door.

Chapter Four

TO THE LIGHTHOUSE

Immediately, the wind filled with packed cold snowflakes, hit me in the face. Brace yourself Bridgette it's a short walk home and even shorter to my destination. The wind didn't let up and gusts of molecules hit my eyes with a stinging sensation that I had to blink away. I held my packages close and smiled a close-lipped emotion of love. I was coming to see my love. Kyle would be so happy I was sure of it.

I had dinner for him and a cold one to celebrate Christmas Eve in the lighthouse. What was I thinking? I had no time to second guess myself now. This was my plan and I was following through. He said it ended on Christmas Day and according to me that was midnight. What's thirty minutes I thought?

I wondered what he had discovered.

The snow had drifted across the road and built a few three feet high drifts against the fence. The road was still clear though visibility was low. I couldn't really see more than three houses in front of me but of course I knew the way there. I walked and I walked with music in my head singing carols of the season. The temperature had dropped just like mom had said it would. Mothers know everything, or do they? Did they have a sixth sense, or just elder knowledge having lived longer than us young adults?

I saw the curve in the road and right after that I'd make a left and walk through the parking lot right out to the spot. I could hear the roar of the lake with waves crunching at the shore. Only two cars passed me and then a truck came by. It was Johnny's. He slowed. I crossed the road and headed into the parking lot with the lighthouse a hundred yards away. I pointed. He looked.

"See the light is on."

He rolled his window down. "Call me if you need a ride. I don't want to worry about you. Got it!"

"I got it, okay? Night."

"Night."

I picked up the pace and nearly ran to the point. Suddenly, I panicked. What if he couldn't hear me knock? I'd left my cell phone at home. I shivered. I frowned. Oh no.

I took a deep breath, it was 11:43. I knocked lightly at first. Nothing. Then I knocked harder on the door to the lighthouse. It had a wreath on it with a red bow. How nice. Just then I heard Kyle's voice.

"Who's there?"

"Sweetie, it's me!"

"Bridgette?"

"Yes. It's Bridgette. I've brought you dinner!"

The door opened. He smiled.

I smiled back.

"Let me take the bags for you."

"Sure. Can I come in?"

"Yes. Perfect timing as its 11:45 and that's a wrap for my thesis."

We walked inside and he shut the door behind me. He set the bags down and it was somewhat warm inside. He had a heater, an electric one. I didn't know that he would be warmed by any modern convenience. I guess I didn't know much of what was in store for him.

Kyle saw me looking at the heater. "Bridgette, that was just to take the chill or freezing temperature away. After all, back in the day the men usually had a house to go to nearby and warm up."

"How could they go to a house if they had to be out here in the lighthouse?"

"The keeper made sure the light was lit and did not stay up all night my dear."

"Are you sure? I bet many a ship relied on this back in the day. But we won't ever really know, will we?"

"Records were kept and I've been reading some of those over this week."

"Did you find out any unknowns not written? Do you have something for your thesis, besides being away from your family and me on Christmas Eve?"

He looked away. I didn't mean to be rather curt but it just came out that way.

"It's very lonely and quite disturbing to be by yourself for a whole week. Trust me. It's, I suppose, much like solitary confinement say like a prisoner in jail."

I reflected on my own experience while on vacation one time from college. "I know, I visited a prison or fort in Puerto Rico once and they led us out to the dungeons. They were dark and made of dirt. One could barely even see inside and the space was such you could not even stand."

"I remember you describing that. Yes, except this is a willful solitude not an imprisonment. And I haven't decided if they are more similar or dissimilar. The main difference is one can walk away at any time, but solitude is solitude, and maybe our mind is the key."

"I can see where you have much to write about. Possibly, if a person can be okay with being alone, then survival is a given. But knowing the lighthouse keeper is assisting in important matters must give it a certain energy, or will all its own."

"Bridgette, that's good. I must quote you for my thesis." He laughed. "Come up and see where I stayed most of the time."

I followed him up the stairs that wrapped around and around. With each step an echo surfaced and it felt rather eerie, kind of like Lake Erie. I'm rhyming and feeling giddy, I think. We arrived at the top room. I saw the window that faced the lake. There was a table in front of it with chairs.

Kyle explained this is where he looked out, read and wrote for his research on the project. He had me look up to see the actual light above us in the tower shining bright for all to see. He had a couple boxes of supplies and a makeshift bed with a camping mat on the floor.

"You slept on that?"

"Six nights, one more to go!"

Chapter Five

THE DISCOVERY

K yle set the packages down upon the table then turned to me, his dear girlfriend. He came at me and gave me a huge warm hug, like he had not seen me in over a year or something. I returned the embrace and kissed him hard. I had really missed him, more than I thought I might. Our kiss lasted a good time and then we met with glazed eyes warmed by the antique interior of this magnificent monument.

"I'll bet this is a first."

"What? A kiss in the lighthouse?"

"No. A kiss followed by a Christmas Ale on Christmas Eve in the lighthouse."

I smiled warmly and held out my hand for the bottle, thinking of an appropriate toast. But I didn't need to bother as my Kyle had one prepared. It seemed.

"I toast to Bridgette and myself, on Christmas Eve, may we never be apart at Christmas time again." We clinked bottles and drank to the stories of Lake Erie past and present.

Kyle pulled out the container with his dinner and said, "Let me guess, a perch sandwich?"

"But of course, tartar too!"

He opened a second container and attached was a little note. "For the two of you stuck up in that lighthouse, enjoy my Christmas Eve clam chowder on the house, love, Johnny."

The two of us sat down and drank our Christmas Ale. I tasted the clam chowder, and Kyle devoured the perch sandwich when I realized the other gift from Johnny. I reached into my inside coat pocket and pulled out the journal.

"I have a surprise from Johnny." I showed Kyle the journal as he ate.

"How did you come upon what seems like a very old journal?"

"Johnny's great-great grandmother was at the Maiden Voyage tonight and she heard about you, and me, visiting you and all. Next thing she had Johnny go and get the thing, then leaves before she tells him to give it to me. He almost didn't want to do it."

Kyle stopped eating and looked it over then handed it back to me and said, "Why don't you read it to me while I eat. Let me light a candle and turn off the light. It will be just like the very old days of whatever year that journal is from. Go ahead. You're not spooked are you?"

"Very well. I can do that. And I'm not spooked."

Suddenly, Kyle flipped the on switch to a portable radio he had on the table and music played over the crackly station. Christmas carols played on a station from the next town over.

"Batteries Bridgette, its run on batteries. Remember no cell phones. I complied with the rules until now, but hey, it's nearly midnight."

"She gave me this for a reason, I just know it. First, she patted my hand, said something I can't remember, then drank her white wine at the bar, all the while smiling."

"Now, here you are ready to read something from long ago. I'm in."

Once I handled the old journal and began to open the cover, I became steadier, ready to explore some past. Here it was right before my eyes. The cover was a new cover over the old book. Inside the old cover and written on the very first page was an elegant handwriting *Diary of Sarah Clemons, 1863-1865*. I gasped at the enormity of this. Could it be real?

"What? Go ahead, please read. I'm ready."

"I will. Here goes."

Kyle's eyes were glued to me.

"This is the diary of Sarah Clemons, 1863-1865."

"For reals?"

"Seriously. I should pick a date because I certainly don't want to read this all night long, not tonight anyway."

"Start with Christmas Eve 1863, December 24th. Read that night to me."

"Perfect, I agree. Her handwriting is spot on just like the chalkboards we had in elementary school."

I took another swig of my beer and cleared my throat. Somehow, I hoped this helped him with his thesis, though not sure of anything this Christmas Eve, except I was with Kyle in the lighthouse reading by candlelight. It was almost romantic.

I flipped through the pages with care so as not to tear anything or damage it. It was quite thick and about halfway through the yellowed pages I found December 1863.

Though my birthday was almost a week ago I still had not gotten use to the idea of being fifteen. Was I an adult or still a child? I most certainly do not know who to conspire with anymore when one wants an adventure. Were there no more adventures in life? Here it is Christmas Eve and I was sent to bed early with the rest of the wee ones, while I'm sure my brother and sister, older than me, are merry-making, dancing, and eating, and most likely staying up later than usual. While I, stuck upstairs in the drafty attic on this night of all nights, awake, and have nothing to do but write in this diary book given to me by a cousin who headed on down south a few years back.

"Really, does it say all that Bridgette?" asked my Kyle.

"It does. How cool! It's like veering right into the minds of long ago."

"Letters are so important for looking into the past." The window took a hit from the gusts outside and we both heard it. Kyle looked out and said, "The snow is coming fast and hard Bridgette. I don't believe we are going anywhere this Christmas Eve. Keep reading."

Maybe next year I'll be able to stay up while the rest of them go to bed early. I must ask mother tomorrow or tell her of my wishes. Pretty soon I'll need to get under the covers as the wind has gone afoul and there might as well be icicles growing from the rafters. Let me think of a fire, the warm and sweet aroma from pine kindling, and the red-white hot glow from burning logs split by dad. Yes, that does warm me up. Until tomorrow diary when the day shall bring me all I want and our family's merriment will last the whole day. Night. Bless this home. December 24th at the eleventh hour of our lord. Sarah Clemons

"That's it?" asked Kyle. The wind howled again and all I could see was white. The weatherman would call this a white out. And here we were alone in the lighthouse. At least we had electric heat.

"That was smart to have the electric heat Kyle. Very smart."

"Thanks."

I turned the page of the diary and it was blank. So I turned another page and there was a hand drawn picture on both pages. It looked like a boat with waves all around it. A roughly drawn body was rowing the boat towards another body in the water with waves all around them. I studied it for a while and determined it was a rescue. "That's it! It's a rescue in a small boat."

Kyle stared at me like I'd gone mad or something. "Let me see that."

I paused to eat my clam chowder and warm me up. Kyle did the same after he viewed the drawing. We were silent for an eternity. What were we thinking? How did this journal even exist? How did we, rather Kyle, get so lucky?

"You may just find something here unique, and far exceeding any thesis requirement for that matter."

With the winter storm rapidly piling the inches upon inches of intricate, white heavenly molecules, majestic mountains would surely greet us in the morning, if not tonight.

I knew that when I turned the page I would be off into the past. I was now the seeker of what happened years ago, more like over a hundred and fifty years ago! Incredible.

What if there was nothing that came next. What if it was tragedy? Then this night was surely doomed. I shook my head and decided then, Miss May, would not have given me a tragedy to read on Christmas Eve. It must be good.

Kyle sat back in his chair and leaned against the round wall of the rotunda. Winter winds howled at us and he said, "Read on Miss Bridgette."

The candle flickered, probably from a ghost circling the insides of this old monument, and I carried on. At this moment I'd believe in anything, so ghosts were not out of the realm.

It is now December 25th, though, not morning yet, and I cannot sleep. Diary, you are not going to believe me but I shall retrace my steps over the last three hours. Only then will I fall asleep and wake up to Christmas Day in the year of our Lord 1863.

"'Sarah, Sarah, wake up dear but be quiet. I need your help."

"What is it mother? It's still dark out. It's not Christmas Day as yet."

"I know darling, but you are the very person I need. All the others are in town, down at the tavern, and there's been an accident of sorts."

"Accident? You want me? How can I help?"

"You are so good with the boats, the row boats."

"Okay, tell me."

"Hurry, hurry now but don't wake the others. I don't want them awake."

"All right mother, let's go!"

"I'll tell you on the way and bundle up as it's storming outside. It's a wintry mix of ice and snow."

We ran down the stairs and pulled our boots on waiting for us by the door. Then once outside we raced across the small meadow down to the docks where we kept some boats. Most all of them were out of the water but we kept two docked and tied up for winter use.

The wind wasn't too bad; I was sure I could handle these smaller waves. But where did she want me to go?

"You know where the larger ships come by Sarah? You know that point straight out from the lighthouse? Before it turns into the bay near Sandusky, or heads on to Cleveland?"

"I do mom. We row all the time out there in spring, summer and fall."

"I know you can do this. I've seen you do it a hundred times and many a time you go as fast as you can like a race or something, right?"

"Yes."

"There's going to be someone out there in the water tonight. I want you to pick them up and pull them in the boat. They will be cold, very cold, but alive."

"Momma, you're mad."

"Trust me Sarah, this is your calling from God above. You can do this. You can save these lives and never talk about it again."

I looked at her. She didn't say another word. She handed me the lantern and kept the other one on the dock. She set it on the dock. She was telling me this is your light, come back to it.

I hurried with the lantern and untied the small boat. I placed the lantern at my feet but I would raise it when I got out to the point to look for people. Why did mother have me finding people in the water?

I raced and went my fastest until I reached the set point. A couple waves hit me and they were cold, though, not like the January temperature I remember. I slowed and rowed just enough to circle around looking for something in the water. I decided that I needed to stand up and hold the lantern up, so whomever could would see the light.

I wondered how long mother wanted me to do this. She hadn't said but knowing my mother, I should return with the people or she would set me right back out again.

I waited and occasionally turned the boat. I looked over to the shore thinking I'd heard a horn. Maybe mother was calling me in. Then I heard it again, the faint sound of a moan, I believe. I looked out to sea as far as I could. Nothing. Then I almost fell over with the lantern when the boat shook a bit.

"Hey lo."

"Hello."

I walked to the front of the boat and looked down at the water and staring back at me were two, three, four sets of eyes. In a moment, I realized mother was saving people. My own mother was a saver of slaves. Glory Hallelujah!

"Go to the back of the boat where it's easier to get on. I'll help you back there."

Quickly, I retreated back there myself. I breathed deeply for the safety of us all. Where was my mother taking these folks? How long had they been out here?

I set the lantern back inside the boat, I suppose, so we wouldn't be seen by anyone else. Now that I knew what my mother was doing, I had to be careful for all our sakes.

First up was two little girls, thin and shivering. I wrapped them in a blanket mother had put in the boat and retrieved the two others, a man and woman. I gave them a blanket as well. I told them to be quiet and I sat down and rowed the fastest and hardest of all my life. I had precious cargo and I knew that I needed to get them inside and warm, else we would lose one of them like we did back in 1860 when I was twelve and my dad's uncle went under fishing. We got him out but it was too late, he'd been hanging on the freezing waters of January nearly an hour or two. My guess is that he froze to death. I hurried. I wanted to do my part.

As I rowed frantically, and fast, I imagined was my mother some kind of hero? I began to think she might be, but not in the eyes of the law. Especially, if they were runaway slaves. People owned them in the south, which was a funny idea to me. My father said properties were large in the south and they needed workers to process the fields. Cotton production increased three-fold and required more labor over a twenty-year period. He said it wasn't right for another man to own another man but that's what happened. Now we were in the middle of a civil war and the abolitionists found ways to free slaves forever, so that no one could find them and return them to their owners.

One way or another my father told me; the slaves will eventually be free. But the cost of war and time involved was hurting both sides.

I could see the dock with mother's light on it. Then it was gone. The mixture of rain and snow came down and we had one last gust of wind before I had us at the dock. All was dark and quiet, then mother and another person, whom I didn't know came forward and helped the passengers off the boat. They rushed the shore showing them to a wagon. Quickly, they stepped onto the wagon, and laid down, mother pulled a cover over the top. The wagon and its two horses went on its way. One would never know what just happened. Then mother came to me and put a blanket around my shoulders. She kissed my forehead and told me she loved me.

"I love you too, Mother."

"Run back up to the house. We must not speak of this ever again."

I looked at her, ready to fulfill her wishes. I hesitated.

"I will tell you if they all make it. Nothing else."

I ran back to the house feeling an enormous sense of pride for my Mother. Oh brothers! Mother trusted me with her most arduous test of the powers to help mankind. I was not a rebel but felt a huge kindred ship with my Mother and kindness towards my fellow man.

"What bravery!" I boasted for the women in this tale while the men were at the tavern on Christmas Eve.

"Bridgette." Kyle hesitated and his thoughts ran quickly but indeterminate he was.

"Yes, Kyle." I returned his statement-question. "You have to admit, that is some bravery on the waters of Lake Erie. It's from an authentic journal. I love it. Shall I continue?"

"Please finish the early morning of December 25th, presumably before the rest of the house wakes up."

My hands are shaking trying to write this after rowing so fast and hard. But I am warm inside and smiling; I shall always remember Christmas Eve 1863. I know now that next year most likely will not be as exciting as last night. My secret. Sarah.

Chapter Six

BACK IN TIME

"**B**ridgette, this is like going back in time to 1863. Christmas is special this year."

"I think so too. I'm happy I'm with you and that we can share this special journal."

"This is someone's personal gift that she keeps hidden and I suspect she only shares with certain people."

"I agree."

"And that special person this year was you. She wanted you to find a keepsake, a special heirloom, and share it with me."

"Kyle, when you read these personal letters or diary, it's as though you are there experiencing it firsthand. She wanted you to find out about a special rescue. She knows it sounds extraordinaire, but you would find it believable."

"And here we are believing in the unbelievable!"

"Kyle, all of history is not recorded, you know that. Many artifacts are either lost or not legible. Here you have a diary, letters from Sara, explaining what she couldn't tell."

"We have to find the answer from her mother. Go ahead, read on."

Mother kept me so busy Christmas Day and the day after, and the next day after, and so on. I don't even know what day this is, but I'm still here. I got a new winter coat, boots and a purse, very stylish. I have no idea where mother had the money for this et all. But she did. And so I was thankful.

January 7th, this is the first time since the New Year I had time for you diary. Sorry.

Today it was heavenly. The air dropped snow particles the size of half dollars. School has been closed since before Christmas, maybe until spring dad says. The lake is partially frozen over as it has been extremely cold. Winter has set in and I just help mom out every day. She looks at me and then away very fast. When will she tell me the slaves made it?

January 21st and the whole earthen existence is a frozen icicle. My mom receives a letter today from her sister's eldest daughter who lives up north in Canada. Mom says for me to make some tea and we should sit by the fire. I comply.

Mother tears open the mail carefully and eyes me in a way that is unsettling. Her face looks pallid for a moment, and scared, eyes that share dread and fear.

She puts the envelope in the fire, burning it. Then she looks at me and sips her tea. She sets the tea cup down and begins to read, no one else is near.

Dear Elizabeth,

Hello dear sister, hope you are well. This mail will probably take three to four weeks to be in your hands, albeit we are only a short distance from one country to the next. I wrote it out as soon as my package arrived.

The hardships of family and winter take their toll, but know that this year our family is especially endeared by a new arrival. We have exploded in size and are forever grateful. And to think I never thought I'd have such a large family.

I miss you and we must get together next summer at the lake. Then I can show you our new arrival and share the wonderful news. I know you will treasure that, since you were such an enormous help for me and my husband, Timothy. He wants Sara to teach him her rowing abilities as well.

All is well. Don't worry about anything. Many blessings. We are blessed by our arrival.

Your sister,

Emily

My mother looked at me and didn't say a word. I paused silently.

I looked at her and knew. This was punishable by death or imprisonment, as I heard my teacher say aloud.

All for saving a life. Imprisonment. Death. Unheard of. Actually, four family members got to live somewhere. I hoped they were happy. I wouldn't say a word. And no one would find my diary. I would do it again for my mother, no skipped heartbeats. Again. I prayed.

I decided to end this diary and start a new one. I love my mother. I will hide this one forever.

Chapter Seven

GOOD DEEDS ARE PUNISHABLE

"**B**ridgette, are you kidding me?"

"What? What do you mean?"

"Is that true that someone could lose their life for helping a slave to escape?"

"It says so!"

The silence hit them both. They felt the history, not just words to memorize for a test and discussion about how bad slavery was in the United States. People risked their lives to help people live a free life. Did anybody know this? Certainly, no one read about how dangerous this might be. After all, abolitionists seemed like gods. Do a good deed and no one will harm you. Right? Wrong!

"Bridgette?"

"Yes Kyle."

"Here, come here."

I cleared our containers of food and cleaned up the table. I glanced out the window and the snow was falling so heavy, I guess the size of half dollars. Then I looked over at Kyle. I was beyond happy that I had come to the lighthouse tonight, Christmas Eve, the "night of all nights" and wondered what was in store for us.

"Thank you for coming and bringing such an amazing story through the journal. That is very special and you are special to me."

I smiled and lacked a word that could possibly match his.

He suddenly reached for my hands as I looked at him. We gazed upon each other with immense emotion in our breaths and stares.

"Bridgette, I don't know when Sara may have met her beloved but I have met mine and want her forever."

I'm stunned.

"I love you." He paused and I knew what was next. "Will you marry me?"

I swallowed and waited for my head to wrap this package in a nice neat bow.

Kyle presented a pretty gold ring. Really, I was being asked to be married. I couldn't believe this. I never ever really imagined this scenario. Never. Never. Ever.

I smiled. No thoughts. Yes. I'm in love. I know I am.

"Yes. Sure I will. I love you, too."

Chapter Eight

CAROLERS CALM

We kissed for a quiet eternity, then hugged in a locked embrace. My eyes were closed and I felt happy. This is what happy feels like, being loved, being wanted, and being appreciated with hope for the future. My eyes were wet with a happy flood. I immediately felt that Sara was so loved by her mother that the gesture and trust placed in her likely lasted her entire life. How wonderful.

Kyle heard them first. "Listen. Listen, Bridgette. I believe we have company. Let's go see."

I followed him down the circular stairs winding around the lighthouse interior. We made it to the door and we could hear them more distinctly.

Kyle opened the door to a cold gust of frigid air which enveloped us. We walked out towards the shoreline and right there with a light snow falling was a beautiful and holy sight. Men and women, our friends included, dressed warmly with long coats and boots, hats and gloves, too, sang a familiar Christmas carol.

"Silent Night, Holy Night. All is calm. All is bright." Kyle and I held each other close. Our first response might have been to share our wonderful news, but we gazed and kept our happiness within as we looked at the scene before us.

This beautiful night at the lighthouse was extraordinarily divine! And by divine I mean meant to be. Some things are naturally occurring in life, I realized, and with some courage we can achieve our personal dreams and futures.

I looked around at the beauty of the night, the stillness set in now that the wind was dying. Kyle and I smiled at our friends and wished them a Merry Christmas.

It was at that moment watching the carolers move on going wherever they wanted I realized that Christmas dreams come true, for me, and even Sara back in the 1860's.

The End

By Kim Troike

Chapter One

First Glance August 2005

anielle felt rather reluctant as the train left the station, it being the farthest one north heading south. The warm rush inside her disturbed her, as she shifted in her seat. Yes! Why? Oh, why must there be a good-looking guy in her airport-shuttle train? Her quick glance told her very attractive, as she stole another look. She checked her watch again and the real time was an unimaginable 6:07 AM. How is this possible? She couldn't even begin to comprehend where her thoughts were headed as she was still figuring out her whereabouts.

Danielle remembered because this flight was so early in the morning, she'd applied no make- up, and forgotten her hair entirely. Why hadn't she fixed it? She needed to think of something else, lest she steal another glance in his direction. The view out the window afforded her breathing time as the train sped to the airport. Dunwoody … Buckhead … Decatur …

Downtown … and finally the destination: the Atlanta airport. She slowly realized this would be a long ride as she and this dark-haired, extremely handsome, man were the only persons on this train.

She made a quick call to Mom and Dad. They were probably having their morning coffee in bed she thought, and then checked her gear. She surveyed the black suitcase; it was standard with handle, wheels, and typical for all passengers these days. Her travel bag held books, make-up (later she thought), snacks and of course her black purse with airline tickets.

Many an August month she had spent in Atlanta and just when July could not get any hotter in Hotlanta; August came right through the front door. *Shut it you may* she thought but the heat followed you, wherever you went. There was no escaping. Must have been why they invented sweet tea with lemon, she mumbled to herself! If you were not in a swimming pool or the lake, make yourself some tea, sit on the porch and make conversation. A smile curved her lip as she perused some leftover memories at Lake Lanier. She'd shared many good times with her sister while boating.

Outside the window, Danielle could see the magnolias in bloom, with their very large white blossoms on enormous trees. The South was always blooming with something, every month, every season; it would tell you what month it was in case you forgot!

"Downtown Atlanta … Little Five Points," the voice of Marta spoke out as the train stopped. A couple of travelers boarded, most likely for the airport and this seemed to startle Danielle back to reality.

She read her book as there was nothing left to do, and decided to get breakfast at the airport.   The Summer Olympics in 1996 had helped to transform this airport into a world class international transportation mecca, so she could get just about anything out by the gate. She had come to Atlanta so many times she could not begin to count. Quite possibly, just maybe, she missed it more than she realized.

Chapter Two

ATLANTA VISIT APRIL 2005

anielle, I just love these short, sweet visits from you. Just like old times!" said Michelle. "Finally, you are moving forward in school and to be a teacher, how wonderful for you."

"Only my third career, sister, but at least I'll get a job," Danielle mused. "Oh, Michelle, I just can't wait to get a job and start teaching. Did I tell you, I think I'll be doing fourth, fifth and sixth grade Math, Reading, and possibly Science?"

"Georgia really needs teachers, good ones, to pull us up the academic ladder! I just don't understand why we are always at the bottom across the United States?" Michelle put her thoughts to words. Where were the answers to this question? Nothing had changed according to the standing of that order in her twenty years in Georgia.

"A few years ago we had such a shortage they were paying people to go back and get a teachers' certificate, as there was a critical shortage when the population exploded in Georgia, specifically, Atlanta. Your timing is perfect. Where do you plan to look for work?" Michelle asked, hoping she might return to Atlanta.

"I'm just not sure what to do. I must first get through school, and then decide. Ohio may not have any openings because jobs are tight and teachers hold on to them." Danielle informed her sister.

"I'm so jealous that you will have summers, holidays and weekends off," Michelle said and sighed. "I worked so many Christmases, anniversaries, birthdays and weekends! My last job held banking hours, nine to five: no holidays, weekends, call or night shift. Outpatient recovery was a nice way to end my career, I must say. I wonder why I never thought to be a teacher." Michelle pondered this, momentarily. She was so happy for Danielle with her new career.

Didn't't big sisters look out for their little sisters? She thought. Don't they try to make sure their life turned out grand and happy? At least she wanted to see her fulfill her dreams, whatever they might be. Michelle often reflected upon that saying 'you have your brothers and sisters around much longer than your parents.' *Truly they hold an important place and vast amount of time in your life!*

"Okay, I'm changing the subject," Danielle stated, matter-of-factly. They settled out on the back deck, it being a Friday in early April. It was warm and surfaces were coated, with the yellow pollen that invades the South like a light yellow jacket. The gorgeous dogwoods were in full bloom, this first week of April, as were the azaleas. Dryness in the throat from this multitude of blooming allergens could be washed away, with an ice cold beer; which they enjoyed on this Friday afternoon.

"I am so glad it's over; I'm done with relationships! Yes, grateful that I did not overlook the jealous factor. He had to know where I was at all times, which made it extremely difficult to be myself," Danielle exclaimed.

"Sorry that ended, and so mixed up like it did. I really thought he might be the one," Michelle said. She'd never had someone be jealous or possessive and thought that *definitely could be a problem.* You'd most likely try to keep reassuring them that all is okay.

"I thought so too. He just didn't believe me, no matter what I told him." Danielle remembered.

"There is probably something inside, like your inner-self telling you it's right or not. Everyone says you'll know when it's the right one; take the reverse of that and you should also know, when it's not right," Michelle said thoughtfully.

Danielle smiled. She knew everything had turned out for the best. But going through the turmoil last fall, showed her how devastating a breakup can be. The result of that emotional drain left a physically slimmer sister.

"To Atlanta and all the good times I've had here!" Danielle raised her glass.

"I have to say the lifeless, hopeless and teary eyed gal that visited me last time is gone,"

Michelle said thankfully. "I believe he knew himself it was not going to work, and that is why he distanced himself from you; so in essence, he did you a favor. Although, no way could you see that then."

All the questions of why's and the angst were gone now. There was life brewing back inside. Danielle, and of course it always helped when one became trim to give a little boost to the ego.

That and maybe a lesson or two was about the only good thing that came from a breakup. Next time a person might try, and weed out, that quality which one distasted right away. Then again, everyone on the planet who's been there, done that, says 'honey, you'll know when it's the right one.'

"It's time for music, and we must make the dinner plans." This visit Danielle had brought Mom and Dad with her. We were going to have a fabulous weekend with cookouts and celebrations of Spring and Easter!

Chapter Three

MARGARITAS ON THE FRONT PORCH

randma Audrey sipped her margarita. After all, she was not a tea-toller, but rather one is good and two's her limit. Audrey Patterson was trying to decide the color of her drink in hand. Was it lime? Was it chartreuse or perhaps citrine? Everything new these days was citrine, which was divine!

"I can't get over this weather; it couldn't't be more perfect. I'm so glad to leave those frozen icicles back in Ohio; I heard they might even get a blizzard today," Grandma said loudly. Grandma was a slender, nice looking lady who golfed twice a week and took very good care of herself. Everyone agreed. Many new Southerners were transplants from the north. Hardly anyone was from here. When you met them, you noticed their accent and usually the pattern of conversation flowed to where they grew up. Michelle's neighbors were families from many states including California, Illinois, New Jersey, Tennessee, Louisiana, and Ohio.

Kelly, a friend from Tennessee held the pitcher of margaritas and said, "Spring-time is the right time for a party on the front porch! Who needs their glass refilled?"

April and May were the most glorious months down South, and May, of course, was Michelle's favorite. By May, the yellow pollen was gone; fresh grass and leaves on trees painted a green palette in the lightest of hues. The beautiful lavender colored wisteria, which climbed trees, had come and gone as had tulips and other bulbous flowers. The flowers had bloomed and now growth took its rest before the hot months descended upon the land. Michelle loved May and wished that month lasted longer down here, with days as clear as a bell and doors left wide open. Soon, May would be here, but for now the *dogwood festival* was here at Piedmont Park, thus showcasing the South's glorious spring.

The little porch party was just what we everyone needed: a little laughter, a few friends, family and jokes, all from the master story teller …dear old Dad. He always found a willing listener, usually, but not always, a female who waited on his every word. In the end the female, wide eyed with rosy cheeks and laughter, followed his punch line with 'are you kidding me?' How does he remember so many jokes? Practice just might make one perfect.

Grandpa to the kids, but Dad to Danielle and Michelle was a good looking man. He bore a striking resemblance to Paul Newman with white silver hair; he was sharply dressed, and full of George Carlin type jokes, ready at a moment's notice. Paul Patterson was well liked, wherever he went. His daughters thought he had wit like Mark Twain. Apparently, in his youth, he was voted best dressed and that remained with him to this day. He was a hat guy, too, especially in the cooler weather.

Today, he was ready for the party and he had a brand new audience to impress! There he was over in the corner with Kelly, as she listened very intently.

"A husband and wife are at home and the phone rings. Ring. Ring. Ring. The husband

answers, and says "How the hell should I know? I'm not the Coast Guard!" The wife says,

"Who's that?" Dad continues with "the husband looks over at her above his glasses with raised

eyebrows. Some guy wants to know if the coast is clear!"

Dad smiles and gets his next one ready, while the people around him roll in laughter.

"Two guys bragging," Dad starts off. "Did you ever get drunk enough to even kiss your girlfriends belly button? Other guy says, hell, I've been drunker than that!"

Kelly rolled her eyes and laughed. She excused herself to go get the refill pitcher of Margaritas.

Watching the kids run and play, sliding down the grassy hill on cardboard boxes, was one of the most enjoyable things to do. From this front porch one could see they had a huge hill for sledding. The kids did not need any snow or sleds as flattened out boxes proved worthy of a fun fast time. This was sledding Southern style! While they watched them expend their energy, the adults talked and caught up.

Laurie the hostess asked Danielle, "Are you dating anyone Danielle? Do you still see that guy you brought here last Christmas?"

"No one serious at the present time," Danielle answered. Mom and Michelle looked at each other with confirmed smiles of she's over him and moving on.

Dad mingled his way to the table about the same time more citrine colored drinks filled their glasses. Again, he found his opportunity to tell some jokes.

"I just found out I was bisexual, you know…my wife said if I want any more sex I had to buy it." They giggled, shook their heads and prepared themselves for more.

Dad, once again started up "In honor of Joe Smith at a retirement party, the speaker said Joe was a horny guy all his life. When he was seven he went to see the little girl's father and talked to him about his daughter. The father said, 'What will you do about money?' The kid said, 'I get three dollars allowance a week.' The father said, 'Where will you two live?' The kid said, 'I've got a tree house. The Father said, 'How will you take care of children?' The boy exclaimed,

'We've been pretty lucky so far!" exclaimed Dad. Half the fun was his jokes and the other half was to see how many he could keep telling.

Laurie, the hostess, came out and announced the food was ready in the dining room per *buffet style*. Michelle excused herself. "I had better go find my children and let them know the food is ready."

Heading for the basement, her eyes glazed over the buffet in the dining room, and shortly thereafter sent a signal to her stomach of how hungry she'd become. Most of the boys had congregated down in the basement, huddled around computers playing war games. The younger girls and boys were playing throughout the house a game of hide and seek or mommy, daddy, and baby. Some things never change. There had been a time when she raced upstairs to see what was the matter only to discover playtime consisted of them role playing and the crying baby was make believe. Being a kid was great she thought, filled with play and friends, no wonder why time passed so slowly when you were young; you filled it up continuously, not worrying about a thing!

By the time the adults made it to the buffet, the children had descended upon the table and deleted the piles of chicken nuggets, pigs in a blanket, cookies (yes, cookies are always the first to go), a few carrots and cheesy potato casserole! The beautiful spread was so appealing you just didn't know where to start. Everyone had brought one of their best recipes or a brand new one for taste testing. This delightful spring day was no ordinary feast but rather a delightful celebration between friends.

Also on the menu was strawberry-walnut, spinach salad made with vinaigrette dressing from scratch, straight from a Southern cookbook; pulled pork for sandwiches, the requisite spinach artichoke chip dip and desserts filled out the rest of the table.

These parties came together like family Sunday dinners from a bygone era, a Norman Rockwell picture from America's past, a **sweet relish for the pickled life they crave**!

Easter Sunday came way too early as Patrick, Elise and Erika descended the staircase rapidly in search of Easter eggs. Empty baskets in hand, ready and wide eyed; they raced around frantic like, as James and Michelle became amused. This would last maybe five or ten minutes, then they would check to see if the Easter Bunny put any eggs outside. *Watching the race for eggs is like observing certain characteristics in your children,* thought Michelle. Personality traits straight from the womb such as: who runs, who walks, who's content to let others pass by, it's all right there before your eyes. Easter service at church, a food buffet and a live bunny to hold filled out the day.

Chapter Four

DOG DAYS OF AUGUST

Once again, Michelle, headed for the train station via the highway to pick up Danielle for the weekend. This would be a short visit from Friday night until early morning Sunday. She thought about the coming weekend and what they might be doing. Danielle always added a certain joy or spirit with her presence. The opposite was true also, when Danielle was quiet the rest of the house became silent.

Springsteen belted out a tune from the eighties on Peach 94.9 FM as Michelle took the big turn off 400 South into the Marta Station. She was running a little late so she pulled up to the *Kiss Ride* as Danielle was already approaching. Good. Perfect timing. Lovely.

August was pretty much unbearable, dog days for sure in the South, and today was no different. Danielle voiced for both of them, "How in the hell did they survive back then?"

"Honestly they must have just stood still, all summer long or went swimming in the nearest lake or pool," Michelle said. "Remember the clothes like long dresses, hats, and boots that they wore? For sure they just hung out, talking about the weather and wishing for the ice man."

Danielle agreed and looked at her own bare legs.

"The kids are so excited their Aunt Danielle is coming to town again. Maybe it's you or maybe it's because you bring them gifts. What child doesn't like presents?" Michelle exclaimed.

"That's my job!" Danielle gave a simple retort. "I might add a fun one at that!" That's when it occurred to Michelle, it was a fun job to be an aunt. Probably along the lines of being a grandparent.

"Dani … el! Dani … el!" shouted Elise, running out to greet them as they parked in the driveway. Erika followed right behind. "What did you bring us?" Erika asked the question.

"Presents, do you like presents? Wait let me see, who's who," said Danielle as she studied their faces. She took a giant leap. "You're Elise and you're Erika!" said Danielle smiling, when she guessed right. Settling into the family room for a while, everyone relaxed. "Where's Patrick?" asked Danielle. "Is he at his second home, his home away from home?"

"Yes, he's over with his second family, the one with the three boys." Michelle exclaimed. "My friend, their mom, and I are actually going to swap and do an exchange of overnight sitting. She's thrilled because she'll have the girls and wants some girl time since she has all boys. She plans on crimping their hair, doing their nails and being girly like."

Michelle allowed her dazed mind to think about how nice that might be, twenty-four hours without the constant responsibility. *Once you have children and you get used to that, you forget what it's like, to just be yourself.* She thought about that quietly.

Sweet, thought Michelle, as she rinsed the dishes and loaded the washer. James grilled burgers and made sweet corn for dinner, along with shell pasta and Marzetti slaw dressing. This is how it's supposed to be, family enjoying good times and laughter together. Patrick ran to get the dessert from the fridge, a special strawberry cake from Publix.

"Yummy!" cried out the kids. "I want ice cream, too."

After dinner the kids took out the Mousetrap game and the adults played with the kids, then they all watched television letting the dinner and drinks settle.

Saturday morning, they discussed the plans for Saturday night. Patrick's friends' mom, Susan, and a few others would be coming along for a girl's night out. The idea was to go out to Buckhead, a lively area of

Atlanta. Susan offered to be the designated driver and it was all set, until the rain came pouring down. Then plans change quickly. Suburbia became the destination. First to a restaurant, a tapas place and then to the bar with a live band. Michelle tried to be upbeat, however, rarely going out meant this was a disappointment as they were not going to the best   places in town. *Boring was the word* she thought if not for the company. They made the best of it even if it was slow and somewhat lifeless out there in the burbs.

Susan questioned her about dating, discussing the online scene. Nothing had really amounted from that, in fact; one was a rather dreadful surprise. They all chided in about dating and the days of 'It's Raining Men, Hallelujah!'

Tiring of the place, and not wishing to listen to the mediocre band. They departed at 1:30AM. Michelle could hardly believe she had to get up and be at the train by 6 AM. How did this happen? After all, these were not the hours of a mom with three children under the age of seven. She was used to sleeping in on the weekends and definitely not going out to bars. The only reason for getting up early on the weekend was to go to a little league baseball game, football game, soccer, basketball game or church. Then again she would do anything for her little sister.

So her final thoughts before closing her eyes, and her head hitting the pillow hard were *nothing ventured nothing gained.*

Danielle had set the alarm and awoke Michelle. Danielle was use to this; she being the energy girl. Always on the go ever since childhood; nothing had changed. Michelle knew she would head back to bed after dropping Danielle off; she just had to make it there and back.

She could smell the Vanilla Nut coffee brewing that she'd set to automatic at 2 AM. With that she poured herself a mug and headed out for the ride to Marta.

Once again, Michelle found herself saying goodbye to her sister.

Chapter Five

JOHN TO THE AIRPORT

*J*ohn arrived at Marta per usual, like a man on a mission. He's got somewhere to be and needs to be there, already. He reviewed the past weekend making sure he'd accomplished everything necessary, before flying on up to Pennsylvania.

He'd been so upset Saturday night at his boss for mandating this trip to Pennsylvania. He just didn't think going on a Sunday, predawn, was a good idea, even though his boss assured him all other flights were full. Reluctantly, John booked the flight and he would visit his brother on Sunday.

In his mind, he reviewed all the details of his recent chores; he'd cut some wood, stacked it neatly, cleaned some gutters, cooked some chicken on the egg Friday night, and finished eating it Saturday night. This thought made him swallow and touch his stomach ever so slightly. He had locked everything up, called and reminded the neighbor gal to take care of, Woody, the dog.

Brittany, the petite blonde who lived down the street would also pick up his mail. She was always checking on John since his wife divorced him a few years back. Brittany and her husband

Keith, had five kids. One of the daughters resembled her dad and two of the boys were the spitting image of their mom. John spent time with them occasionally on Fridays on their driveway, when work was finished.

He parked his silver truck and took his bags from the back seat. John was excited now as he would get the chance to see family in Pennsylvania. His brother lived there and kind of acted like the protector since his dad died. Life was getting better, maybe; maybe not. Rather he was just getting used to the fact that he was alone. He had a roommate who lived in his basement, that he never saw. Definitely, he was not as lonely as in the beginning, but damn it, he thought, *something was missing!*

Quickly walking out to the train, he saw a brunette gal in a tight black skirt, looked to be about his age. He noticed that she seemed to know what she was doing, while he wasn't quite sure how all these tokens worked. Hell, why not just follow her and sit on the same train? Maybe he'd find out where she was going, and where she was from. This was the most northern train station, so unless she was visiting, she had to live up here, too.

Chapter Six

THE MARTA TRAIN RIDE

anielle hurriedly tried to remember how long the ride was to Atlanta Hartsfield airport; she could not even muster this information out of her tired brain cells. *Thank you, Jesus,* she thought, *that she did not have a hangover.* No. No. No. That would have made this unbearable. She nodded to herself, smiled a closed lip smile and with that glanced over at the dark-haired guy, sitting by himself. He was the only other being on the train and with that done, she felt her shoulders relax. She began to read her book and also wondered why she was attracted to him, if that's what it was.

James Patterson's Lifeguard, the library book she'd checked out was absorbing any thoughts, while the train slipped through downtown Atlanta. She needed a hot tea, ever so badly, to get her perked up a bit. School entered her mind briefly as it was two weeks until finals, then student teaching this fall. The home stretch was in view. Daydreaming about being a teacher and instructing in front of class excited her and made her nervous, too. Closing her eyes, she pictured a scene filled with wonderful little children, 6th graders, raising their hands to answer the question before them.

"Wow, so many of you seemed to have completed your homework assignment!" Marybeth murmured lightly.

It was then she felt a tap on her shoulder and she looked up to see a smile across the face of the dark-haired guy. He said, "Hey, it's time. We are at the end of the line. We're at the airport."

"Oh, okay, hey thanks. Guess I was daydreaming…" she said surprised and shook her head a little. Packing up her book, purse and suitcase; she departed the train for the plane.

He asked, "Where are you going and what flight are you on?"

She responded with, "Cleveland flight #967 and you?"

He responded with, "Erie, PA flight #412." Smiling, he added, "Ok, have a good one."

First up, she thought, *ladies' room, then a long trek through the airport.* She'd get some tea and breakfast.

Danielle remembered, as they departed, something important, from her travel agent days. Atlanta to Erie always went through Cleveland with a layover. Hmm… Maybe she would see him again.

John left and mumbled something to himself, an expletive, damn, under his breath. He gave her one more look, and smiled, thinking he longed for someone special in his life. Then he changed his thoughts to his brother, and the good times he would have this week once he got to Pennsylvania. John journeyed his way through the airport, never occurring to him he would have to go through Cleveland to get to Erie with a layover to boot.

Chapter Seven

HARTSFIELD JACKSON AIRPORT

The English breakfast tea warmed her interior and now the outside began to soften. A quick call to Michelle and they held a brief conversation. Danielle did inform her about the guy on the train, and that he probably was going to be on her plane to Cleveland. A smile appeared and stirred her to face what lay ahead, whatever that was. Her stride was quick now with her head held high and her hair accenting a beautiful face and shoulders. She saw as she approached the gate the dark-haired man with thick tan Carhartt shorts, a yellow shirt and white tennis shoes. He was turning and noticed her walking towards him.

He took it all in like slow motion, a beautiful gal with shiny brunette hair in a tight black, short skirt and orange top walked toward him. Quickly, he told himself, to ask her name; must not forget that! He thought to himself, *one fine, hot looking babe.*

"Hey, I'm John by the way." He added quickly. "I found out I am going through Cleveland to get to Erie. I remembered that after you walked away."

"I used to be a travel agent. Actually, my mother owned it, an agency called **To the Moon Travel Agency**." Danielle added.

"Cute. Do you have a name?" John asked. *I must get this now*, he thought to himself.

"Danielle, Dani for short!" She smiled now and liked the way things were moving along.

At this point, the conversation began to center around personal matters, finding out the all-important items, such as married or not, kids, jobs and where they lived. They agreed to talk in Cleveland, while they waited during the layover. Danielle phoned Mom and Dad and made sure she had some time at the airport before they retrieved her.

Chapter Eight

CONCOURSE D

The plane arrived at Concourse D in Cleveland, the farthest one out. John waited for Danielle and escorted her through the airport. Danielle found a bench where they could sit and talk during his layover. He had so much to say and only an hour. He talked about work, kids, and where he was going. Danielle reciprocated with her school schedule and work.

They sat at the corner window looking at planes coming and going. The anticipation of conversation and learning about each other was definitely brewing heavily for both.

The smiling, acknowledging, and questioning seemed to be taking control and had a life all its own. They exchanged emails and a few polite responses. Danielle went curbside and John went to his gate to catch his plane for Erie, Pa.

She scanned the curb for a light green Cadillac and began to feel a little elated. Yeah, that was nice! Stepping in the Cadillac she stated, "I just met a nice guy!"

"Oh yeah?" Mother's replied.

"Where from?" Dad's asked.

"Where did you meet him, on the plane or in the airport?" Mother asked.

"No, I met him on Marta!" Danielle exclaimed. "He's from Ball Ground."

"Is he going to call you?" Mom asked.

"I think so." Danielle was fairly certain.

Chapter Nine

FIRST PHONE CALL

Sunday night came after the day of traveling, and spending time with Mom and Dad shopping at a nearby mall. Walking through the door to her home always felt great; now though, Danielle must get ready for school tomorrow and do some laundry. Her condo was fixed with nick knacks collected from numerous shopping trips with Mom; perusing the North Coast gift shops for Paris items such as cafes and Eiffel tower. Maybe, therein lies an unfulfilled romantic dream of love. She smiled as she thought of John, wondering if that newly opened door would amount to anything.

Listening to her answering machine for messages, while watering the few indoor plants she had, she made her way to the computer to check emails. The very first email, the latest one, read

Danielle,

I made it to my brother's. We golfed all day in a tournament for my brother who died several years ago, a tribute to his life, in memory of him for his family. Hope you had a good day with your family! I enjoyed talking and will call you tomorrow night.

Bye,

John

Wow. Smiling she went to bed. Monday morning was going to be great.

Danielle was ready for this class as she had prepared all last week. She couldn't wait for student teaching to begin. Enthusiasm releases that freshness from teachers which children crave. They want you to be more excited than they are, that way it must be important, fun or worth knowing about! Danielle was one of those types with abounding interest and vivacity.

"How was it today? I cannot believe you are finally student teaching!" exclaimed Michelle. She was thrilled for, Danielle, that her first day was over and eager to see how it went, and if she liked it. Liking kids and teaching a class of thirty or so, could be way amazing, or a hair- raising experience.

Breathy on the phone, Danielle had much to say, "Today was good, we covered the Math, Social Studies, and Language Arts. It's unbelievable how one or two will try and run the class; talking out of turn, throwing things and actually getting up out of their seats when the teacher is talking. I'm going to have to instill a certain respect for adults, which they do not have. Nowadays, you cannot touch a child in any way, even to direct them."

"For real? You can't touch like to give encouragement on the shoulders or arms; possibly a job well done with a pat on the back? No way, in nursing touch is paramount to healing and consoling as it soothes, and restores us physically and mentally. No wonder, we are so removed from our children," Michelle said with astonishment. "I guess with lawsuits teachers have to protect themselves." She began shaking her head wondering quietly; what is wrong with this world? She would want someone to console her child, while away from her during the day.

It was Michelle's philosophy that next to the parents, the teacher held the most responsibility and time with her children, therefore, the third most influential human being to them. This was why teachers are valuable, and important right along with teaching the curriculum.

"Call you later, just got home and have things to do," Danielle said.

"Okay, catch you later!" Michelle hung up and smiled.

Ring. Ring. Ring. Danielle ran for the phone wondering who's calling, *must be mother*, she thought.

"Hello. It's John. How are you and how did the first day go?" John asked eagerly.

"Well, it went pretty good. I must say. A few kids acted out, but all in all, okay," Danielle stated. "How are you and what did you do today?"

"I had some meetings about new equipment with the company; which we'll be using very soon in Atlanta. I'm done for the day and going out with my brother and his wife for dinner, a wonderful German restaurant, they tell me. What are you doing for dinner?" asked John.

"Mom and Dad are having my Aunt and a few other ladies over for dinner. I'll join them. Aunt Marian, and I have sort of a special bond. She never had any girls, just three boys, so

I'm her girl. She buys me presents for my birthday and has given me special tea cups, saucers, and jewelry over the years. My Dad is making perch from one of his fishing trips on Lake Erie this summer. This is one of his special meals he does, all by himself. Mom will make a side dish or two," Danielle said.

"I want to come to your house for dinner. I'm salivating right now. There are two things I totally love, well, make that three. I love fish, chicken and beer! Ha ha." John meant every word. "Catching fish, grilling chicken, and drinking beer, or is it chicken, beer, and fishing? Wait for sure it's beer, fishing, and chicken. You get my point?" He laughed.

"Well, there is plenty of all of that here!" Danielle said assuredly. The conversation flowed with John discussing his two children, what grade and sports they participated in. Basketball was big, both were good at it. Danielle would come to realize talking about his children brought him great joy, as he had missed out on much of their lives.

Danielle informed John about her, including her sister Michelle who was married to James in Atlanta. They had three children, whom they adopted late in life, completing their family. Michelle was a nurse and stayed at home caring for the busy family. James, a hard working dad was a good time guy that liked to have fun! He worked in medicine for as long as she could remember, a perfusionist, straight from Ohio State University. Patrick, the oldest, was seven, smart, and fairly independent. A kid with blue eyes, blond hair, skin that tanned so dark in the summer. He had cheeks like Winston Churchill. Danielle used to say Patrick was hiding squirrel nuts in those cheeks. Elise and Erika were about six now, born sixteen months after Patrick, and the sweetest little angels anyone could ever imagine. They weighed just under five pounds when they were born and fit on your arm from wrist to elbow. John took the family leave act, three months off, with work guaranteed; the act Bill Clinton passed while in office. This helped, Michelle, get adjusted as no family lived nearby.

Danielle told John how much fun and enjoyment she has gotten, from being an aunt to these wonderful kids. She informed him that Michelle always praised the birthmothers for their courageous act of love and kindness, by placing them for adoption. This was a selfless act and it helps families to become families. She went on to tell him some the latest mispronounced words. Blananas and panacakes was Elise's very funny terms for food, and the sweet angelic voice of Erika as she said the word cookie, made you melt.

Danielle went on to say that she loved coming to Atlanta to visit. Their house on the hill had a finished basement for entertaining with a bar. Whenever she came to town, they would invite friends over and gather with kids running around, just like they grew up with their cousins and cookouts of long ago.

John really began to feel at ease with all this talk. It seemed like the more they conversed, the better he felt. He felt a sense of comfort like he could trust Danielle, and trust was such a big issue in relationships; if people could have that then the relationship could go further. This pleased him the most, and he was beginning to feel that with Danielle.

Chapter Ten

SEPTEMBER PHONE CALLS

Upon returning home after six days gone, John, checked with his neighbors, retrieved his mail, and asked them how Woody faired. He couldn't help but spill the beans. So about two seconds after he started talking; he let them know he met a girl on Marta on the way to the airport. Brittany started with some grueling questions, sizzled with "Is she hot?"

"Woman, your mind is always in the gutter, always thinking sex!" John smiled. "I'll fill you in later as I've got to go home and give her a call. She lives in Ohio."

"All right John! It's about time you meet yourself a woman, man can't go so long without one ya know," Keith muttered to John sipping on a scotch and smoking a red Marlborough.

Mail in hand, John went out back to see Woody. Woody had his own large area, a dog house with a fenced area. Occasionally, he slept out back or on the back screened in porch. A chocolate lab, Woody was husky and friendly. He obeyed John and loved kids. John's last girlfriend had given Woody to him as a Christmas present, then in January they broke up. John had a dream about a week before they broke it off. He envisioned a girl driving a silver car all by herself, no kids, no ex-husband and just going out with some friends looking to have a good time. He wondered after he woke up if someone like that existed. He fed Woody, let him in the house, tonight it would be Woody and him sitting by his wood stove. He lit the fire, opened a beer and dialed Danielle's number.

"Hi. I'm so glad you called, was just thinking about you and wondered if you made it back without any problems?" Answered Danielle.

"Yeah, no problems, glad to be home but I had a great time with my brother. He's such a cool guy! His kids are grown up and moved away. The quaint and quiet little town of Waterford has a golf course along the LeBeouf Creek and eventually feeds into the Allegheny and Ohio rivers. It was a French town, complete with a fort and then the British came and subsequently George Washington, as it was a part of the French and Indian Seven Year War." John supposed he might have been trying to impress Danielle with that extra bit of information.

John was in his 44th year, doing well at work; he had built a log home with Duane's help. He'd lived there now four years as his wife left two years ago with his children. Somehow, she couldn't handle the area and found someone else. It had been extremely difficult to be alone, and not see his kids, coupled with the burden of child support and losing half of his retirement.

He just kept busy and tried not to think of it. Bitterness crept in now and then, he wasn't sure if he'd ever be over it. It made the acid in his stomach burn. Duane occasionally gave him some chew for times like this when you just needed to forget. John, a peaceful man was quiet for the most part; loud when he wanted to be and very hard-working. He kept busy all the time. He put another log on the fire and settled back with another beer and kept talking. He found that he could talk for hours about every little thing.

Danielle was to turn 45 this December and had never been married, ever! She had never let anyone get close to proposing. Something she must have known about that the timing or the person was not quite right. A couple of times it looked, according to Michelle, that things might just happen. So, she encouraged her. Michelle would say, stupidly, what do you have to lose? Get a divorce later; it will be like a breakup. This was reckless, but you will have walked down the aisle and tried. Michelle realized how idiotic this sounded, but said it anyway.

Danielle told John of the online dating she did with a couple of dudes, and realized it was not for her. One dude came in his leather studded, motorcycle gear; walked in and took one look towards Danielle. He said 'this is not gonna work.' *Go figure*, she thought. What the hell was he looking for? Maybe he wanted blonde hair and leather?

Sandusky was Danielle's birthplace with Huron her hometown, both on the water. This Vacationland paradise with summertime activities and destinations brought lots of people here. Boating with island hopping was a big draw and these places catered to the crowds with singers and bands of all kinds. Lake Erie is the shallowest of the Great Lakes, therefore the roughest when the storms hit. The famous Edmund Fitzgerald freighter went down in a 1975 November storm and Gordon Lightfoot sang a song about it, *'The Wreck of the Edmund Fitzgerald.'* Danielle grew up one house from the beach and lake, with a pond out back. Ice skating in the cold wintertime was a favorite pastime for the kids. The lake area was blessed with the snow effect every winter.

Fast and sweet describe Danielle, always in a hurry or at a complete standstill. Her accomplishments were many as in education and degrees. She had a Bachelor's Degree from Bowling Green State University, obtained in three years, in Human Resources Management. High School was also completed in three years as Danielle was definitely on the accelerated plan. A week after graduation she was bound for Houston, back in the 80's when it was a boom town. Retail seemed to be the jobs she obtained and managing stores was her forte as she worked at Victoria Secret's for many years in Atlanta and achieved success at these places. Later, when mother bought a travel agency, she took a course in travel and became an agent, moving back home and operating this with her. The two of them worked well together, traveled at a moment's notice using discounts before the high gas prices hit.

Danielle realized the time and said to John, "Oh, it is late, time to make some dinner! Have you eaten?" They decided to keep talking and make something to eat. Smiling, they cooked together, then they ate dinner together … over the phone.

John explained to Danielle, he did not have a desire to go to college when he was younger. He enjoyed working with his hands building things, working, fishing and massaging a woman's body. He said the last part real slow and smiled. He was sure she was smiling too. Parting with goodnights and sleep wells; both languidly went to bed.

Just a few days later, they connected again and related more of themselves to each other. John rambled on about his family with five boys and no sisters. He had grown up in Erie, a coastal town on Lake Erie, named for the Native Americans which inhabited this area before the French arrived in 1753. The French built a fort to defend themselves against the British, called Fort Presque Isle, this means 'almost an island.' It is a piece of land which jets out into the main body of water. The French abandoned this fort to the British in 1760, three years later the French and Indian War was over. John, of course knew all this like the back of his hand. There was so much history here in Ohio on the Great Lakes with the Native Americans, the British, the French, and the Canadians with all the waterways including rivers and lakes. Many a battle was fought here.

Continuing on, John relayed that two of his brothers died of heart attacks and one died in a car accident. His mother died at an early age from lung cancer, his father remarried a very nice lady, his stepmother. After he got in high school his dad and her would go to Florida for the winter and leave he and his brothers to themselves. Probably this made him more independent with a can do policy which John abides by. He played some basketball in high school, but found he loved to fish. An uncle or brother would take him out on Lake Erie. This was a peaceful and enjoyable thing to do, away from everyone. John also found out he loved to eat the fish he caught. He sure hoped he was not boring Danielle with all of this, but she chided in many a time that her dad and grandfather were fishermen, both owning boats. She even had a grandmother who lived on an island and rented out boats and sold bait to fishermen. Indubitably, her family loved fishing and ate Lake Erie Perch, whenever they could. This pleased him to no end; how did he find someone who seemed to be similar, single and gorgeous!?

One evening after a couple hours on the phone the discussion of what they wanted out of life came up and John talked about how important her family is, especially her Mom and Dad. She had spent a lot of time with them these last ten years as they were companions and friends; and of course the laughter from Dad always added life to the party. Certainly, many a smile and good time was had when they got together several times a week. The festival at the boat basin in Huron every summer, the islands and their home on the lake were some of the most enjoyable things to do. Huron, also named after Indians which inhabited the area, was the small town where Danielle grew up. The French gave this name to these Indians meaning boar's head, or bristly coiffure on the males, and also rough and boorish. The Huron name was important as usually, this name meant islanders or peninsula dwellers. These Huron Indians cared for their children, believing they were the tribes future, so importance was placed on education of the young. Trading of beaver and selling these to the French, which then sold the furs to Europeans, was highly valued and done regularly. The Huron Indians were fishermen, hunters and farmers, hence, all three brought in goods-a-plenty with fish, bears, deer and crops like corn, beans and squash. They were a colorful tribe using vegetable and mineral dyes mixed with sunflower oil or bear fat to make red, black, violet and green face paint. They for sure used many a layers in the cold winter months with leggings, skirts, moccasins, deerskin shirts and fur. They painted designs and fringed the skirts, as they were a creative, decorative lot. Danielle was sure these

Indians had rubbed off on her, as she loved clothing and loved to shop for clothes. *Oh where was this conversation going,* she thought as it sounded far-fetched? This is one of her pastimes she informed John, shopping! She told him she envisioned herself shopping for him and dressing him with some special items. She smiled, just the thought of buying John clothes and getting the right color for him brought her a rush like none other. She felt excited, maybe even thrilled. John listened to her thoroughly, as she informed him of her area and its history.

He thought to himself that her family sounded very nice and he would like to be around more family gatherings. He told her he liked the idea that she had not been married or had kids. "I know that sounds egotistical and maybe I'm a son of a bitch, full of bullshit; but I'm smart enough to understand, I don't want any drama. Sorry." He let it out, sighed so big and could sense the release of frustration as he breathed. She could not imagine all the drama with marriage and exes; she'd had it with boyfriends and that was enough.

In the end it seemed, they both wanted companionship and love with a sense of trust, and to share their families with each other. Sounded pretty sweet, like the tea Danielle enjoyed, freshly brewed, bursting with just squeezed lemon and a packet of sugar.

A few days later Danielle arrived home to her condo and at the doorstep was a bouquet of lilacs, daisies and anemones with a note that read:

To cheer you and let you know my heart is thinking of you! John

She put the beautiful yellow daisies, light purple lilacs, and blue anemones in a French blue vase, placing it on the counter in the kitchen; she poured herself a glass of merlot, smiled and drank the fruity wine. She felt a bit blissful.

Chapter Eleven

BALL GROUND VISIT

The whirlwind continued and two weeks later Danielle was on a plane bound for Atlanta. Mother's encouragement felt warm and genuine and Michelle was so excited for Danielle. John would pick Danielle up from Marta and drive out to his place: a log home on two acres. *Who in the world lived in a log home*, she thought?

"Hopefully, he's not an ax murderer!" Michelle exalted. Did she realize how trusting she was being? Michelle, continued her thoughts; *I suppose how else do people connect when they meet on a plane? I guess they go to one city or another.*

"Remember, Danielle, how you got to his neighborhood and if it seems shady or you become scared or whatever; call me and I'll come to get you, immediately!" Michelle instilled in her sister.

"Michelle, I appreciate that. It seems far out in the country, but I'll remember how to get there and will call you from my cell phone." Danielle tried to reassure Michelle and it was not working. John parked the silver truck in the parking garage at North Springs and rode the shuttle to the airport, just like he had two weeks prior. He picked her up at the gate and carried her bags for her. Riding Marta again, only this time together as a couple seemed a bit surreal. They chatted up small things, smiling at one another. John and Danielle talked about the weekend ahead and went over all the ideas both had come up with to do. They could take a visit to Helen, one of Danielle's favorite towns in North Georgia, attend a cul-de-sac party at her sister's, travel to Dahlonega, and meet Johns close friend Duane.

John and Danielle drove on route 20 to Ball Ground; some of this was familiar to Danielle as she'd driven route 20 to get to I-75 en route to Ohio. However, now they were turning on country highways with beautiful farms, and horses all around; she saw tractors, red barns, rows of crops with little tiny houses, trailers and the occasional brick mansion. Other houses of a bygone-era such as the Victorian homes had pieces lining the roof edges in need of paint and repair, made one wonder, how old the place possibly was? The land presented had gently rolling hills of green pastures and fences with the sun shining down saying, here is God's land just for you. People still live out in the country, where the air has a different smell. John turned right saying, "Here's Duane's property. He has the log home up there in the woods with about 20-25 acres right there".

Danielle could see an old brown wooden fence outlining the huge corner with a few horses grazing on grass. Next they turned into the neighborhood and Danielle saw large spacious lots with beautiful homes next to a lake. Smiling, she thought, *I'm out in the country but this seems different.* It was rather pretty, serene, and very peaceful. She probably wouldn't have to call Michelle. She was feeling more comfortable by the moment.

Pulling up into his driveway, Danielle, could detect a little pride in his voice as he began telling her about his place and what he would show her. Her eyes drifted off to the woods and beyond as his voice faded about the building of this log home built by himself and his friend Duane.

He went on about the time frame, how they constructed it, and where it came from. She did hear the part that he had built this place for his family, picking out this beautiful lot with Duane's help. Yes, it was his pride and joy next to his children.

The inside was like no place she had ever been before, as John had spent the last two days cleaning and it showed. The wood floors were gleaming as were the beautiful wood beams. The feel of all the wood warmed her heart and made her smile. This place was so beautiful and different; it felt like she was on a vacation in the mountains. The smell was a clean light wood scent. John reminded her it never gets very dirty, since he is the only one living here. Room by room, they lingered. Danielle was so amazed she had to remind herself to take a big breath.

The interior was of a golden color and looked freshly cut; John told her it remains that way even over time. John grabbed a couple of beers and they continued their way to the family room, where off to one side sat a large wood stove. He put a couple logs inside and lit them showing her and explained how it worked. He said he uses it to heat the place in the winter as it does not get that cold in Georgia.

"So what do you think?" John asked.

"Awesome, smells like brand new!" Danielle managed to say. John turned into Danielle and kissed her right there next to the stove. The first kiss was here and it did not disappoint!

After a trip to Wally World in Cumming to retrieve supplies for the weekend; they went to Jacks, the local liquor store. It was the kind of place where you run into your neighbor and purchased your brew and rum. A quick bite at Johnny's pizza and they headed back to John's.

The plans were laid out with a trip to Helen, the Alpine Village in the north Georgia Mts., which happened to be one of Danielle's favorite destinations in the fall. Labor Day on Sunday would be at Michelle's and James' cul-de-sac party, barbeque and buffet with all the neighbors and then a return plane trip on Monday.

As soon as all the groceries and beverages were unloaded the neighbors and their five kids showed up. "Hey John, what's up? We've come to meet your new girl!" Brittany exclaimed.

"Well, here she is. This is Danielle from Ohio. This here is Keith, this is Brittany and this is two of the five kids, Savannah and Tyler." Meanwhile, Savannah and Tyler raced around, and played with Woody a bit. Danielle thought Savannah and Tyler were cute kids with a fairly thick southern accent. She asked them their ages and questions about school, and had to ask them to repeat a couple things. Some southern accents, usually true southerners, have very thick drawls.

Meanwhile, they relaxed, had a drink and exchanged niceties. Danielle found out their nicknames were Cookie and Red. Keith had reddish, blond wavy hair and was a tall large man with a mustache. He smoked Marlborough reds and drank scotch, although Marybeth wasn't sure what kind. He traveled for business and looked as though he had been enjoying a few meals out to restaurants. Cookie as she was called, maybe a reference to a sweet treat, preferred white wine or champagne. John said he would explain the champagne later to Danielle, he smiled and walked away. Brittany 'Cookie' started chatting about, Dixie and Trixie, her boob job.

Danielle knew her eyebrows were raised as high as they could go, but she was astonished this was the conversation having just met Brittany. They chatted lightly about her and John meeting on the train and when she and him would get together again. Danielle noticed how tiny Brittany was and yet how boisterous her voice could be. She came from a true southern town, and was a bit theatrical. She had charm, wit, and boldness. She had long white blonde hair and large deep set green eyes. Her husband, a southern good-old-boy, with a flirtatious eye and noted swagger when he walked, could keep you entertained for hours. Danielle smiled and thought these people would make for interesting get-togethers. They were larger than life, larger than she was accustomed.

John loaded up the stove with his cut wood and put some Stevie Ray Vaughn music on. Danielle and he settled on the light camel, leather sofa side by side looking at the fire. She felt she had arrived home.

Chapter Twelve

DUANE'S VISIT

The knock on the door woke both of them up from their slumber. "Oh no, dang, it can't be!" John jumped out of bed and raced to put his clothes on. He looked at Danielle and gave her a big smile. "You are about to meet Duane, I'm pretty sure." He hurried to the door and sure enough, just as he expected; there stood Duane with a cheek full of chew.

"Mornin` … boy! Can't wait to meet her. She up yet?" Duane spoke briskly as he walked right in and headed for the coffee pot in the corner of the kitchen.

"I have not made the coffee as yet. I'll do that right now, just for you," John said quickly. John was actually looking forward to this meeting, Duane meeting Danielle; he really wondered and wanted his opinion. Duane always gave his answers straight up, *to his own self be true*, thought John. They had been friends a long time and Duane had certainly been there for him.

So with no preparation, Danielle made her entrance wearing her clothes from last night. She walked into the kitchen and greeted Duane with a bright, sunny hello. "Hello, I'm Danielle."

"Duane. Glad to finally meet ya, thought maybe John was going to keep ya, all to himself." Duane spoke with a heavy southern accent, thick and slow on particular words. His smile shifted slightly, and he winked at Danielle giving her a once over. His smile beamed big and bright in John's direction, then he offered a welcome to Danielle to the fine state of Georgia, and especially, Ball Ground. He filled his mug and exchanged with John, what he doing and then he was gone. He told Danielle he would see her again as he was looking forward to getting to know her and she would be able to meet his wife.

John informed Danielle, "Get used to that. Cause he does that every weekend, even an occasional evening during the week."

Danielle did not mind as she was up early even on the weekend. She realized Duane was important to him. She wanted to meet him and get along. She had not known what to expect. Duane was middle age, probably fifties or sixties, with blondish-white hair in a ball cap, thick jacket and work boots. His weathered face and hands gave away his years, working a farm with cattle, chickens and haying, gardening too. He had twenty to thirty acres and rented out the field to others where they kept their horses. He had a few chickens, therefore, fresh eggs were available from time to time. He also lived in a log home.

Danielle was putting together this picture. *Hmm*, she thought, *maybe like father like son.* She would give that more thought in the future. It crossed her mind you just didn't meet those true Southerners anymore, down here in Atlanta; then again she reminded herself she was in Ball Ground.

John filled her in after Duane left. Duane had lived here all his life. In fact, John told her that at the Publix down the road, on Rt. 20, there were pictures of his family on the walls. One in particular was of a schoolteacher, with her children walking to school on a rural road. Ball Ground only has about 1000 residents. It is very near where the Cherokee Indians used to play stick ball, a game similar to lacrosse. Local legend has it that this is where the name Ball Ground came from. Large fields were needed for this game, so along the streams and rivers the Cherokee

Indians would gather to play. One of the rivers is the Etowah, just down from my home he explained. There's a lake too, Danielle pointed out the window, across the street. He told her yes, that's it. You can take Woody for a walk, he told Danielle.

79

Chapter Thirteen

HELEN, GEORGIA

Today, Danielle and John, would venture out to familiar territory; she showered for the trip to North Georgia, specifically, Helen. Every time she traveled to Atlanta in the fall she found herself in Helen, during Oktoberfest. It was her favorite thing to do, maybe it reminded her of Autumn in Ohio with the leaves, their color changes and cooler temperatures. Possibly it brought out the passionate side of herself, a place which held many beautiful memories. The Alpine Village, a re-creation of an old German style town in the North Georgia Mountains is in the Appalachians, not the Alps. Thirty-five years of celebrating Bavaria style Octobers draws many tourists from September through November; as folks walk along the cobblestone alleys, shopping and dining in the old-world style buildings lining main street. The Chattahoochee River runs through Helen and in the summer is filled with brightly colored tubes as people chill out! They lazily meander through the town letting the current carry them to a distant destination.

Christmas is also alive and busy through December with lights, carolers and Christmas shoppers. There is so much to do but the main draw is the German food and beer! Cars line up on the strip just outside town, and it can take an hour just to get in town on a weekend day in October. Danielle just loves this quaint little town, now she and John were coming here for the whole day! She could not wait to share this with John.

Driving into Helen with the windows down, feeling the warm pre-Autumn air and listening to a Bryan Adams CD, Danielle thought nothing could be better as she looked over at John while he drove. It was still September so the main road wasn't too crowded. The traffic slowed just as they passed the local winery and store. Danielle said "I'd like to go there and shop inside, maybe on the way out of town."

"Danielle, I've been here only once, a long time ago. I'm excited to taste the German food and drink some beer!" John said and smiled at her. He was thinking to himself how lucky he felt right now. They found parking and began strolling along browsing the shops, listening to the music and smelling the awesome scents floating in the air. "Mmm, I can smell the brats cooking right now!"

They both spied the restaurant with the deck hanging out over the river, and decided to eat lunch there. Danielle ordered a Reuben and John asked for the special bratwurst & knockwurst combo with the red cabbage. One could look out over the balcony onto the Chattahoochee River and see the revelers floating down the hooch at the end of summer. Music could be heard coming from the square in the center of Helen near the fountain. It was a live

German Band. John and Danielle could see the street and bridge from their table and watched the crowds crossing as the rafts floated under the bridge. Conversation at lunch seemed to focus on food. Danielle said she always orders a Reuben and that she should try something else but never does! John told her he loves chicken and eats it almost every day and would have ordered it, but he had not had brats in a while and, oh well, it was October. He was German, so why not!

Next up was some Alpine shopping, and shopping was Danielle's favorite thing to do whenever … wherever … period. In and out they went, perusing little shops, candle shops, fudge shops, music box shops, Christmas shops, clothing shops, and then, finally a historical family name shop. This shop held their attention for some time. As soon as the line cleared, they approached the counter and asked the lady to look into John's last name, which was Yeager. Danielle had looked hers up many years ago, on one of her trips to Helen. The attendant showed John his last name and he read the whole thing.

"Wow, unbelievable, how can this be? It's so true!" he exclaimed in amazement. Shaking his head, over and over, from side to side in the negative; he could not believe what he was reading. "Danielle, this is incredible; it says here Yeager…the man in charge of the woods. The man staring at the woodshed!" John chuckled to himself, as she didn't know him that well, yet. *She would find out*, he thought to himself, *is this fate or what?*

Walking hand in hand along the boardwalk, John and Danielle, were getting closer as the weekend progressed. Spotting some kids with ice cream, they opted to get a cone and continue window shopping. Coming to where the horse drawn carriage rides were parked, John spoke up and said they should go for a ride. This surprised Danielle as she had never been for a ride. She smiled, finished her cone and was ready.

Stepping up into the carriage, sitting down facing the horse, the driver spoke up "My name is Karl and this is Sunflower, the 1st and oldest horse, up here in Helen. We've been together now with the carriage rides for 11 years, and she could take us through these streets blindfolded all by herself. She knows them that well!"

Sitting back and enjoying the ride, the driver went on story after story about himself, his horses, and of course Helen. He seemed to know everything! *Sunflower was a big horse almost like the Clydesdales from the Bush commercials,* Danielle thought to herself. The hooves were gigantic and before she had stepped up she noticed the body of Sunflower was as tall as herself. Danielle began to relax and nestled into John, touching his shoulders and finally rested her head there. John took a deep breathe, relaxed looking all around taking in this moment and planting it in his brain. He was not eager to depart from this carriage as Sunflower turned the corner. The owner gave Sunflower an apple and a carrot after their departure. John tipped him and they were on their way again.

The clock tower in the center of town chimed ringing out three o'clock, and both decided to head back to Ball Ground. They needed cookout supplies for dinner tonight. "You are in for a treat tonight cause

I'm going to cook you some chicken on the egg!" John said gleefully. She told him she wanted to see how this magic Green Egg worked.

Pulling up the drive they could see Woody out in his pen, so excited running hurriedly and wagging his thick brown tail. After unloading the truck, Danielle decided to give Woody her attention, while John fired up the egg and got the chicken started. Woody was a chocolate lab with some English bull in him. Short statured with a gorgeous shiny brown coat, his head and shoulders were wider than typical of Labradors. He was friendly! Leashed up and ready to go, Woody walked Danielle down the long drive and out into the neighborhood. Walking on the

grass which met the blacktop road, she took a deep breath and sighed. As evening neared, the temperature dropped and made for a fine evening indeed.

One could always breathe better in the Deep South when the temperatures cooled, humidity departed and the sun set! She believed this was going to be one of those evenings! Her shoulders gave a little shudder, which made her heart skip a beat. A feeling overcame her as she looked out over to the lake, the one John talked about. The feeling was as though she had never left Georgia, and everything was coming together now, after all these years. Smiling, she accepted this idea and continued looking at the beautiful lake. Tall pines and hardwoods framed the homes with a hint of fall colors mirroring on the lake. A small rowboat was tied loosely to a three foot dock waiting for the next folly. *It was time*, she thought, to get back to John.

Joining him on the back screened-in-patio, where the precious egg was cooking the chicken; they enjoyed a cocktail, rum and coke with twist of lime to be exact, and John showed her his precious, Green Egg.

"This here is how it's done mademoiselle, Danielle!" Chuckling, John, turned the chicken breasts to the other side. "This baby here cooks it just right and these chips add so much to the flavor, you are gonna love eet!" John added.

"Smells good," Danielle said sniffing the area. Standing very close now she wasn't sure if it was the chicken cooking on the egg or the scent of John's neck and shoulders.

John turned and smiled, setting his drink down. Their eyes gazed upon each other and locked there. Pulling her to him, he was never more ready as he gently put his lips on hers. His hands moved over her shoulders and down her back bringing her body forward to his. Desire swept over him in a flash, and he felt an electric current in this kiss. He wanted to taste her and keep this kiss going as it was so sweet, and hot, at the same time. Their mouths equally entwined sharing this desire only increased their sense of wanting; this embrace brought a closeness they both had been looking for. Releasing the kiss, they held each other close.

Chapter Fourteen

CUL-DE-SAC COOKOUT

The Labor Day cookout would be on Sunday in the cul-de-sac with Michelle's family. This would be a big production with everyone helping to do their part. The men would gather all the patio furniture needed from selected houses in the morning using a trailer and deposit them in the circle. Someone in charge had already pre-arranged the menu and written down what everyone would bring. Large food tables were also set up and some speakers for music; one of the neighbors had decided he was going to perform tonight with some *git er done* jokes. About 50-60 neighbors would eventually show up tonight, share food, drinks and good times!

Friends began arriving around 5 PM with their potlucks and chips, dips, side dishes, desserts and beverages. Looking for their specific tables and chairs that the guys had set up earlier; most would need an umbrella about this time of day to elude the hot sun. Earlier in the day the kids had participated in a few bike races, skateboard races and several rounds of Frisbee golf for the older boys. One of the father's flew his remote control airplanes overhead for all to observe and landed them gently on his driveways' pavement.

Danielle and John arrived at Michelle's and James at 5:30. James asked them for their drink order then they all headed to the bar in the basement.

"Hey, ya all, this is nice! What is this mahogany? And this lip on the bar? Very nice!" John loved (him) some wood and he was determining what kind this was with the glaze on the bar top.

"I believe it's alder with a stain as it resembles mahogany. How about a black and tan for a beer?" James asked thinking he would serve him up his specialty.

"Sure. I'll try that. What's in it?" John didn't think he'd had that one before.

"Guinness is the black & Bass is the tan! The Guinness is poured over the Bass." James

showed him what he was doing. "There you go cheers!"

"Cheers!" John responded gladly.

Danielle and Michelle headed up to the kitchen and gathered up the side dishes, etc. "Danielle, he looks like one of our cousins. He has that dark haired Irish look; very cute I may add." Michelle couldn't wait to give her opinion, as she was happy for her sister. She thought to herself, 1st impression is a good impression. James and John stayed in the basement a good while passing some jokes back and forth.

"Mom, when are you coming out? Mrs. Kim wants to know!" Elise inquired running into the kitchen.

"Very soon sweetie, tell her very soon," Michelle said. "Danielle, see if the guys are ready". Danielle retrieved the guys from the basement, although they looked so comfortable where they were sitting and talking. *Male bonding in action* she thought; she hated to pull them away.

The men came upstairs and appeared reluctant, like we were just having a good time. Everyone made their way outside, found the table and chairs, and settled in with introductions. The kids were running every which way, dancing and hula hooping to the music, and playing hide-n-go seek amongst the houses. Music was blaring, people were smiling, and candles were burning; the smell of barbeque was in the air. It was a party!

Back at school she was student teaching for the whole semester; there would be no visit now for months. This would be a real test, especially for a beginning relationship. In school all day, and lesson plans to be made at night; Danielle had little time to ponder what John must be up to. Already finished with two careers, teaching seemed logical and a way for Danielle to help children whom she loved. Her studies at Bowling Green State University in education were focused on the elementary or primary levels up to 6th grade. So many changes she felt had occurred, since she was a kid. Times had changed also; children came from a vast parenting pool of divorced, single parents, step parents, gay and married. Students were vocal, talking back to each other and teachers. Teachers these days had to learn how to deal with these aspects alongside the curriculum. Touching was another issue in our very sterile society. No touching, not even a pat on the shoulder or arm for reassurance. No religion, no religious music and no Christmas. This was just a different world from her years growing up in the Mid-West.

One comment, Danielle, would find rather daunting "I can get you fired! My mom will call the principal!" When she heard this comment, she thought *where does that come from?* Fired? She is only student teaching. *Where is this lack of respect, learned,* she thought? Is it at home or in school, maybe TV or daycare? She called Michelle and mulled this over with her. Michelle had a hard time believing what she was hearing. She gave it some thought and could only come up with empowerment or lack of. These kids need to have some sort of control mixed in with lack of parenting as to setting boundaries and showing others respect. *Wow,* she thought, Danielle has a tough road. The thought made her laugh out loud. What if a patient said to her, I can get you fired! Stunned would be her response or maybe a call to the family.

Chapter Fifteen

GEORGE FROM LONG AGO

Unexpectedly, one cold night, Danielle answered the phone and it was George, an old boyfriend. He wanted to meet up with her as it had been awhile. Hesitantly, Danielle said yes.

"Good, I'll see you at 8:30 inside the Sandbar," George confirmed.

"Okay, see you then," Danielle said.

She thought to herself, *this will be fine*, as my life is moving forward and John will be coming to Ohio for Thanksgiving in a couple weeks. I can see George and tell him about John and finally close this ancient chapter. *Easy peasy*, she thought to herself.

The phone rang again and it was John. They talked but she found no reason to tell him about seeing George tonight. She didn't really want to tell him she was going to meet someone she could have married at one point in her life. The timing never happened; both were at different levels at different times. Danielle felt it totally unnecessary to bring this up at this time.

Danielle pulled up to the Sandbar and walked in to meet George, he was wearing black jeans and a red shirt. He waved her over and stood up to greet her. He smiled and thought she always looks so polished and happy.

"Hey, Danielle, how are you?" George smiled and kissed her on the cheek.

"Great, and you?" Danielle asked smiling.

They found themselves catching up easily, smiling, joking and informing each other of the past two years, as it had been that long. George had finally gotten his degree and was working in his chosen field, Occupational Therapy. He was beaming, then again George was always a happy guy, one of the things she had loved about him. They ordered pizza and beer. Danielle was enjoying the old familiarity of George and all they'd shared. The spark was still there, maybe it would be forever. This night is just what she needed, feeling fabulous and entrenched in

George's company; it was easy to see why they had dated and lived together such a long time ago. Maybe, she thought, *that's why it didn't work, because they had lived together and not made a commitment.*

George asked Danielle if she was dating and she told him about her new boyfriend. He smiled, and said, "I knew something was up, something was different about you. Are you in love?"

"Maybe? Not quite there, yet. But … probably, yes." Danielle stammered.

"Oh, we never quite got on the same plane, same time, thing going, did we?" George said, reluctantly. He leaned in and kissed her so gently on her cheek, both of them smiled.

Chapter Sixteen

PORK TENDERLOIN WITH PLUM SAUCE

It was decided without question Thanksgiving would be in Ohio with Mom and Dad. November was one of those unpredictable months in the north with a very late autumn or the first winter snow. Mother Nature could bestow the soft and cold, white flakes or a gale force wind upon the land. The first snow of the season was a wonderful blessing, especially if it came at Thanksgiving. While everyone sat around stuffing themselves inside, later they could sit in a chair and watch the tender flakes and dream of Christmas.

What did come at this time of year were November gales, very strong winds with even stronger bursts making it treacherous on Lake Erie at this time of year.

John had arrived by plane then drove to Bowling Green with Danielle and waited for her while she finished up a class. It was nice to be together either driving or sitting in her condo. "Michelle and James are driving up here with the kids for the holiday also," Danielle said to John.

"Great, that will be nice. Are we all going to have Thanksgiving together?" John questioned Danielle.

"They are going to James's parents and we will have dinner with Mom and Dad at my condo. Later, we'll meet up, I suppose for some football on the tube!" Danielle said.

Michelle and the family had arrived quietly a couple of days ago and visited relatives in town. Thanksgiving fell on her Birthday this year and when that happened the day was extra special.

Looking through the blinds the white flakes of snow fell down softly and made for a quiet moment. *No it couldn't be,* she thought. And what time was it? Michelle could not hear a sound nor smell any coffee aroma; she knew it must be very early as it was still dark outside. The snow made it a touch brighter, street lights reflecting on the snow. Smiling, she thought to herself, *this will be a very special day indeed with the magic that snow brings.* The children will have smiles and joyful glee in their voices! Last night was a typical November night: chilly and bleak, no leaves, and no life, anywhere. She knew when she got up in a few hours most likely the ground would be covered; a white blanket just waiting for little angels to come and play.

Everyone in the house eventually woke up, and grabbed a cup of coffee, then looked outside at the beauty and quietness of the falling snow. Somehow it elicits a feeling of wonderment for the charm which nature invokes upon us. Makes us feel glorious. Michelle just couldn't believe the snow was falling on her Birthday! She gave a quick thanks to the Lord above. Patrick, Elise and Erika were quickly devouring their breakfast to see who would get outside first to play in the snow! After breakfast sitting in her robe, Michelle decided this was as good a time as ever to go play the piano.

Mother had a fine piano, a grand piano which sounded magnificent, especially when you played with the pedals, which always maximized the sound. Michelle had learned to play organ but could play piano using chords for the left hand and notes for the right. She pulled out the Christmas book and there it was 'Over the River and through the Woods.' She couldn't resist and

played it loud. Poor Mr. Shupe, her organ teacher, who taught her so happily but she never practiced much. "I was never prepared, hardly practiced, but I learned. Bless him!"

The Christmas tunes came next. She couldn't believe all this was coming back to her, like she had played last week. Before long James came out and gave her a surprised look. She heard him say to Mom, "She hasn't played in ten years!" Nothing like a compliment when it comes from the one you love and it's overheard, seemingly therefore genuine. One by one the kids came in with a shocked look on their faces, "Mom is that you? I didn't know you could play like this! You're good." Oh, this day is perfect! She loved all of it and played with a smile.

Suddenly, Michelle thought, *time for a change, a transition, it's time for her.* She felt more like herself at this moment than she had in quite a while. *These moments are few in life,* she thought, they catch you and you hold on to them moving you forward.

Simultaneously, the two parties left for their respective destinations with, Audrey and Paul, going to Danielle's condo, and Michelle, James, and the kids going to his parents condo.

Arriving just before noon, Mom and Dad stepped inside with the dessert and a few appetizers. "Mmm … smells good Danielle. Wait, is it the food baking or the delicious smelling candles burning?" Mother asked.

"Hey, how are you doing John?" Dad offered his hand for a shake. "Call me Paul."

"It's very nice to meet you." John shook hands smiling as he met her Mom and Dad.

"Danielle's been filling me in on a few things; feel like I know you both already. Can I get you a beer?"

"Thanks, you have a Rolling Rock?" Dad asked.

"As a matter of fact, we do, just for you!" John said happily. He'd have something to talk about. While they compared brews, Mother and Danielle, went over the menu for the day then set out the appetizers of fresh, raw vegetables. Mom's favorite vegetables served raw were broccoli, cauliflower, carrots and celery. Mom had made a fresh ranch dip for these and brought also some pretzels, crackers and cheese. Danielle poured herself and Mother a glass of white wine and joined the fellas.

Conversation flowed back and forth covering many subjects, including John's mother who died when he was nine. His stepmother, who was very good to him, and whom he loves immensely was still alive as well as his two older brothers. Many times when his father was still alive they had gone fishing together. Mother thought John friendly, very jovial and a good natured man. Dad and he hit it off with Dad putting John in stitches at times with his not so rare, George Carlin, humor.

When dinner was ready they gathered around the table and gave thanks. A non-traditional feast had been prepared, as Danielle and Mom don't care for turkey. The menu was as follows:

Pork Tenderloin with Plum Sauce

Baked Potatoes with Cheese, Bacon, Chives and Sour Cream

Green Beans with Almonds

Cranberry Salad   Apple Pie a la Mode

Mother's Recipe for Cranberry Salad

1-3oz. raspberry jello

1-3oz. cherry jello

½ can whole cranberries

8oz. crushed pineapple

Prepare jello as directed. Allow to gel then add cranberries/pineapple.

Put in mold and refrigerate.

Chapter Seventeen

WINTER SEPARATION

It was snowy and bleak through most of January; Danielle thought she'd seen more white and felt more freezing air than in previous years. The dry biting air reddened her cheeks, cleared and tingled her nostrils every time she headed for her car. A thing of beauty the first week out, but after a few months one grew tired of this great white north. How could people live like this? She wondered. Then it was easier to do her studies, and prepare for class sitting inside when the roads were covered in snow and partial sheets of ice.

She and John talked on the phone or emailed constantly, sharing bits and pieces of the day. However, the more time went on she felt a little desperate that they ought to be together; they were not building that closeness, that sense of familiarity and knowing. They would see each other just once in five months; this seemed almost unbearable. Her thoughts turned to how busy she was with school, finals and student teaching. Right now, though, all she could think of was him. Daydreaming, she recollected his dark black hair, brown eyes and his slender build. Yeah, she laughed aloud, his pants were always falling down, as he had no butt. She would buy him a good leather belt next time she went shopping. Michelle was right; he did look like a Printy. Danielle made some tea and pulled out her book to study. This would be a long winter in Ohio. She smiled to herself thinking of John and Ball

Ground. Just then the phone rang.

"Hey. Girl! What ya doing?" John asked on the other end. And then the two hour phone calls began. They would play music, drink some wine or beer, talk about their days, and each other. They both liked Brian Adams song, 'Have You Ever Really Loved a Woman?' It was to be their song! They both liked Stevie Ray Vaughn and played this quite often. John, she learned was calm and quite the outdoorsman with fishing, woodcutting and taking care of his log home. He was always busy and in a hurry during the day, but at night he sat down to relax or watch some basketball. He really liked basketball! Both of his kids played basketball for high school. He liked watching Le Bron play too! He worked for the same company for 23 years now, a medical supply company, and worked very hard.

Danielle filled him in also on her life, including the present time working for Mother's travel agency, **To The Moon Travel** and going to school at the same time. She had lived in Atlanta for many years and had been close with her sister, Michelle. She'd gone back to school for travel then moved back to Huron to work with her mother. Huron, a small town, had been a refreshing change from the big city of Atlanta and being near family had been comforting. The Travel Agency, had given her many travel opportunities here in the states and abroad. She had joined the ski club and taken trips with friends in the winter time. In the summer the islands, Kelley's and Put-In-Bay, offered many pleasure seekers, boater's and vacationers a destination with music, food and fun!

John had determined that Danielle was sweet and amiable, fast and in a hurry like him. She

could be loud when she wanted to be, witty and a bit sugary, and oh, she loved to shop!

"John, I must go, well, I see it's been two and a half hours. I'm really looking forward to Spring Break when we see one another again. I'll email you my flights with the times. Good night!" Danielle hung up and went to bed.

Chapter Eighteen

SUMMER TOGETHER

Hotlanta! Yep they don't call it that for nothing. Hot, hot, hot and more hot. Sunscreen beaded up to pearly white jewels on your perspiring skin and the only relief besides shade was a dip in the pool. Danielle was used to this when she lived here for ten years but it had been a while.

"Michelle. Thank you, for finding this job for me this summer!" Danielle exclaimed again.

"No problem, it was meant to be. How on earth did it happen so easily? See things are working out for you, Danielle. That's what they say, when it's meant to happen it will, it will be easy and just happen; you don't have to force anything." Michelle issued those words, those famous last words that people believe; but they don't want to hear when it is them. When they want something so bad they can taste it; but they can't obtain it. She knows, cause this happened to her. No matter how hard she tried, she was not to be pregnant, not even after three in-vitros.

She was told God closes the door but opens the window. Yeah. Yeah. Yeah. Only after you live through it can you feel the spiritual blessing, when something wonderful happens.

Danielle was to be a nanny this summer and work for a doctor with two children during the daytime. She was thrilled. The online advertisement had come to Michelle through the neighborhood online press. Danielle, would be right around the corner working and staying with John for the summer. How lucky was that?

Headaches bothered both of them this morning; however, John was not to let that interfere with his amorous feelings. Danielle had been here a whole week and life to him seemed rather blissful. Mornings and nights became a time to express their love for each other. Evenings brought them together with him at the grill and Danielle fixing salads and appetizers. Dinner would often be in the screened-in-porch out back shaded by the tall hardwoods intermingled with pines. Daytime had them each going their own way. Danielle went to nanny two children, and John went off to the hospitals, checking the operating room lighting.

"Good morning dear!" He greeted her. He handed her a cup of tea as she liked it. He sipped his coffee, discussing what they would do as today was Saturday, this meant chores for John and errands for Danielle. Maybe she might even get over to her sister's for some pool time and sunshine with her nieces and nephew. "I'll make you breakfast and if you want you can take Woody for a walk," John suggested.

"Great idea that will get me moving and it feels like the perfect day, sunny, but not hot," Danielle mused. Quickly, she readied herself for a walk with Woody.

"I'll have some eggs ready when you get back. What else do you like?" he asked her.

"Surprise me." She said smiling and out the door she went. She and Woody walked down the winding paved driveway. She looked over at the neighbor's house and kept walking all the way down the road. The noise of a loud lawn mower came from the cul-de-sac direction and she could see someone mowing the lawn in what she thought to be a bikini top. The kids were riding bikes and scooters on the driveway. The man was edging the drive. She then proceeded to the lake and walked around and then returned home just in time for breakfast.

"Mmmm smells delicious and looks even better," Danielle told John as her stomach growled. He'd prepared her some bacon, eggs and wheat berry toast with home-made strawberry jam straight from Duane's garden.

"Did you see Britney and Keith outside?" questioned John. "Doing their Saturday morning yard work?"

"Yes and the kids are outside having fun on the drive," she added.

"I'm thinking we ought to go over and see them, so you can get to know them better." John alluded to Danielle. He just thought that this was probably a good idea.

"Agree, let's go," Danielle said quickly. And off they went.

Rustic log home, if those three words described Brian's place, then quaint cottage

homestead, described Keith and Britney's place. It was white with the large hanging ferns on the front porch, curtain laced windows and tender loving care bestowed upon every view your eyes locked into. The driveway was long, straight, flat and perfect for little kids to ride bikes, scooters and play multiple games. Perfect for happy hours on the weekends, Britney was enjoying a glass of champagne.

"Hey ya'll, how's it going? Wondering when ya would get out of that bed over there and see the light of day." She lingered over these words, smiling at them waiting for an answer. Her lips sipped her bubbly at the rim of her glass, flipping her hair.

"What?" Danielle stammered. Her eyebrows slightly lifting thinking like is she for real?

"Hey. Britney! Britney, how you doing neighbor; how's life treating you?" asked John.

"Well, pretty good, just mowed the lawn and Dixie and Trixie here are a little hot!" she said as she looked down and fanned her chest. "Keith's about done there and then he's going up to the corner to sell the boiled peanuts today for the first time. We'll see how that one goes."

"How are ya Danielle?" asked Keith with genuine regard. Keith was a robust fellow from the South who had worked his way up the chain of command for a lumber company. He enjoyed his scotch on the rocks and Marlboro red cigarettes. He remained faithful to his wife, although, at times he gave off the appearance of a different matter. Sandy blonde, wavy hair that was thicker than a fox's tail in mid-winter, with a mustache to match. Talking with Keith was like talking to one of Mark Twain's characters, maybe the man himself. You walked away wondering, what you really talked about, like it was of some importance but you weren't quite sure. "John treating you betta than his wife thought he treated her?" Keith chuckled. "Being lonesome mellowed him much. I know he's pretty happy right now, cause of you." Straight to the point, that's how Red grabbed life, in front of the bush; no hiding.

"Red, fetch me some ice when you're in the house would ya?" Britney called to him.

"Sure honey, anything for you, Cookie. Need more champagne?" Keith hollered back.

"Nah, I'm good, it's just getting warm out here, especially my drink!" Britney scolded.

"He's gotta go sell the peanuts up at the corner today. We boiled 'em last night, packaged 'em and now, they are ready to sell." Britney explained to John and Danielle their new venture to bring in some extra cash.

"Really? I know people do love those down here. I have never acquired the taste, even though I lived here quite a while," Danielle explained.

"Momma! Momma! Come, see what's eeside dis trayunk ova heear," exclaimed the littlest child, Tyler. His thrill and excitement drew the adults over to view what had his curiosity and enthusiasm. He found a stick and began to poke in the center of a dead tree trunk in the ground.

"Tyler back up, now!" Savannah yelled as her eyes became big and hysterical looking. "It's a snake, a big snake." She backed off as mom and dad came forward. Of course, everyone had their opinion of what to do and who do you think won this one? Yes, momma!

"John, kill it for me! I must not have this creature slithering all around the place with the kids playing right here on the driveway," Britney spoke in the most commanding voice known to her.

"I will let you all handle it as I've got other pressing matters." Red delighted in his departure. He knew John more than capable of handling the snake and taking care of his distraught wife. "After all neighbor, you are the man of the woods, Mr. Yeager."

John ran to his house and retrieved a shovel. Meanwhile, the kids stepped back but stayed the course ready to watch what Mr. Yeager was going to do.

Danielle began an explanation about the name Yeager. "You know, the shop, up in Helen that has the origins of names and the meanings behind them?" Danielle queried Britney. She gave a nod as such. "Well, Yeager means *hunter, the man in charge of the woods.* In the Middle Ages, this person would decide which trees were to be cut down, to control the animal population. John's exact words when he read this were *Oh, My God!* He said this is the truth, you'll see. Now I see."

"I know he probably would just throw the snake back into the woods, but I have to have it gone, permanently, especially with the kids here," Britney said with slight reluctance.

Danielle did understand this and nodded in agreement.

John returned and instructed the kids to go into the garage, and get him a water bottle. When they both ran to get this for him, he procured the large garden snake and proceeded to return it to the woods. It would not be sleuthing about the grounds any longer. "There now you don't have to worry 'bout that snaky snake no longer kids," John uttered.

"Thanks, Mr. John. My momma won't be scared now. Will you momma?" Tyler ran off to find something else to do.

Savannah went right up to John and told him "Next time, you wait for me, because I want to see how it's done; I must see this for myself, ok?" She looked at him patiently waiting for an answer.

"Savannah, are you sure you want to see that, dear?" John asked observing her face.

"Yes, I can take it, I know I can!" She stammered out, smiled and turned away.

"Thank you, dear, so much. I'm so glad you live in this

neighborhood. What would I do without you?" Britney thanked him so endearingly and poured herself another glass of champagne. "To John, bless you!" She raised her glass in toast.

The excitement of the morning long gone, and the chores of the afternoon completed, the couple relaxed and listened to music. Life's good in Ball Ground.

Chapter Nineteen

CHRISTMAS IN BALL GROUND

The email began with:

'My man who stares at the woodshed, I shall be coming down there in five days and I cannot wait. I will be loading up the car and praying we won't have a blizzard before I leave. It has been quite a while since I have driven the trek to Georgia, but know that I can do it as I've done it so many times before. I have stocked up on the Great Lakes Brew as you requested, Dad and I went to Cleveland to their store and purchased it, along with a few other items. It is close to four months now, since I've seen you, and I'm glad it's over. It's been torture and I don't want to ever do that again. In touch soon…..'

John sat at the computer feeling happy; Danielle would be here in five or six days. Thinking about her, and her being here, made him smile. The log home he built for him, and his family, was empty. His mind wandered off to a recurring dream. He typed a quick email back, then made a list to prepare himself, and his home for the arrival of his girlfriend, and possibly, more importantly, a future partner.

Danielle tooled around the kitchen, Christmas Eve morning, preparing for Xmas Eve festivities. Michelle, James and the kids; Patrick, Elise, and Erika were all coming over for the evening. The next door neighbors were also invited so it would be festive and fun. This past week she and John had decorated a live Christmas tree, with ornaments she had brought from Ohio. It looked so beautiful in the family room with the golden wood beams rising up to the ceiling. The wood burning stove emitted a soft red glow and allowed the burning pieces to permeate heat to the great room and kitchen. Concentrating on her recipes in hand, she gathered up the ingredients she'd purchased yesterday and began. Christmas tunes floated from the front room, and she hummed along at intervals. She saw John feeding Woody out back. Then he headed over to the shed; she could tell the next thing up was logs.

This was going to be the best Christmas as she had just graduated from college, quit her job at **To The Moon Travel** and moved herself back to Georgia. Michelle always told her she did things very quickly; surmising this was true, she quickly dismissed the thought and moved on. A quick call to her sister and everything was set for the evening.

Christmas morning John told Danielle he had to check on Woody in the garage and do some cleaning up. Meanwhile, she prepared some coffee for him and some tea for herself. She turned the stereo on to Xmas tunes, and turned the tree lights on. They'd decided they would have a cup of caffeine, shower, and then open gifts.

Freshly baked cinnamon rolls, and another wakeup cup made Christmas morning gain some needed acceleration. Casting their eyes on the resplendent Christmas tree with all the glorious ornaments and ribbons, their hearts joined as one, momentarily with smiles from the eyes.

"Danielle, did you notice the new ornament I bought and placed on the tree?" John inquired.

"Really, where is that?" She asked as she scanned the tree.

"Look up near the top, in front." John nodded in that direction.

Danielle arose to her feet and especially wanted to see what John had picked out.

"Hey, is this like finding the needle in the haystack?" She asked. "Oh, here is one which is not mine. Is this it?" She paused as she saw a gold Christmas tree ornament outlined in the shape of a tree.

He watched her look it over and smiled at her when she looked in the middle.

"It looks special. Where did you……what's this in the middle?" She looked at him.

He looked at her lovingly, and asked, "Would you, Danielle, marry me?"

Silence sustained the pause then she turned, smiled, and said, "Yes."

The ring dangling in the center of a Christmas tree ornament had been John's idea and a uniquely, beautiful one at that.

John removed the ring and put it on her finger. A Christmas Day engagement ring, she couldn't wait to tell everyone. Then she kissed him, and hugged him for a long time.

She'd always loved the south, she thought to herself, and now she would be back here again, and married to John. This thought filled her with joy, and tears fell to her cheeks. She must call Mom immediately and share her news. Danielle would wait until Christmas night to share this joy with Michelle, and her family.

"Hey, guys, come on in!" Michelle greeted them at the door Christmas night. The Christmas afternoon lull was over, and now it was family relaxation time. Sit back, and let the kids play their games, and the adults could relax as the work was over for now. The decorations in all their glory, with lights illuminating in every room was impressive. There were lighted candlesticks in the windows, a radiant Christmas tree in the family room, outdoor lights decorating the house, and a sleigh in the yard with one reindeer, whose head moved side to side which took two days to put up left one feeling rather warm at this most special time of year. "The party is in the basement; we've a small tree down there with the kids ornaments they've made over the years at home and in school. We picked the smallest tree we could find at Big John's lot up at the Plaza in Cumming."

"Look at what your sister got me for Christmas," John bellowed out and displayed the camera, Danielle had bought him. He was acting like a kid and began snapping pictures. Like a kid with a new toy, John did not put the camera down, even when he gave James one of his Great Lakes Brew, a Commodore Perry. "Did you show them what I gave you?"

All eyes went to Danielle, waiting for her to show and tell, and she held up her hand.

"No. Way. Oh, my, gosh! Let's see!" Michelle spoke for all.

Patrick said "Ooh, Danielle, a ring. Whatever is it for?"

Elise and Erika spoke at once. "She's getting married. John is her Prince. Prince John." As everyone surrounded Danielle to view her engagement ring, that emotional feeling of happiness; a once in a lifetime, happening, connected all of them in the room.

"Biting the bullet, huh? Ready again for those ball and chains are you?" James spouted loudly.

Happy barely describes how Michelle felt that night as the party progressed on. Christmas night was always a special night, a solemn ending to a beautiful season filled with love, family and spirit. Knowing that Danielle had finally found peace and love with someone, a bond strengthened by the fact both were seeking, assured her of a closer tie.

Such contentment comes, thought Michelle, *to stroke her own heart as her family has been touched with such sorrowful news, the ambivalence felt rather than spoken.*

One Saturday night in January, about twelve days after Christmas, the sixth to be exact, Danielle and her family found themselves visiting the newly engaged. Duane showed up, and they were all able to meet this special friend of Brian's. He proceeded to tell of the many jobs he

had throughout his life, including being a dairy farmer for many years and now sharing his pasture with horse owners.

"I have always wanted a horse! Every birthday I would blow out candles on my cake and wish for a horse; I mean every one til one year I just gave up on it. I tell my kids now to tell me their wishes or let it be known," Michelle said looking at Duane smiling. He winked back at her, and she thought to herself I like this person; he's got some magic in those winks like he really knows what I'm talking about.

"You want a horse? I can get you a horse. I've got one for sale right now, a Tennessee walking horse. You can keep it at my place." Duane sounded like he meant it.

"Oh, I'm sure it's too much. How much is the horse and the pasture rent?" Michelle was getting excited, her eyebrows were peaked and her ears very keen at the moment.

"I can git you the horse fer six hundred and you can keep it at my place fer a hundred a month." Duane stated matter-of-factly. "Come check it out tomorrow." He winked again.

"Ok Michelle, there's your horse. Check it out." Danielle said.

"He knows what he's talkin about; he's got horses there all the time. I'm tellin ya," John added.

Michelle looked at James for verification of something. He said "You got some money right now; spend away. I don't know anything about horses! I can't help you."

Blame it on the wine, blame it on the time, whatever; it seemed like the right thing to do. So, Michelle told Duane she'd see him tomorrow. Disbelief but thrilled, the kids were so excited.

Once at home James looked up Tennessee Walking horses online and found the information. "Apparently plantation owners from Tennessee blended two breeds in the 1800's, as they wanted a horse that could ride all day over the vast and varied terrain. This breed which was bred in the Southern United States, called the Tennessee walking horse, was known for their running walk and a horse canter which has a gentle rocking motion. This flashy walk can be referred to as 'big lick' in shows. It's a very special horse, I guess."

So over the course of the next few months, they tried their best to become acquainted and knowledgeable about Cindy. She was beautiful and they learned to groom and love her; although they never did learn to walk her like the owner who sold her. He had showed them that special running walk and it was beautiful. Cindy was a biter and the other person interested told them they needed to take control and not let her get away with that. They somehow managed to accomplish that, giving her carrots and apples. Another horse owner at Duane's gave the kids lessons around the field a couple times a week. Duane fed her and they came out three to four times a week, visiting Danielle and John, when they could. Patrick mostly liked to chase the cats and check on the chickens and their eggs they hatched on the farm; whereas the girls wanted to be around Cindy. When possible, they brought friends to see their horse and the farm. The farm experience was a light in their eyes and no one complained when mom rounded them up for the visits each week.

Duane was there most of the time to assist and help. He even offered Patrick some chew one day, with that wink in his eye, and then spat it out in a purposeful direction. Patrick tried his riding skills but did become discouraged one day when Cindy bucked him off with speed. All of this was fun and then some; but when Michelle had time to think about it she became nervous thinking about the dangers of horseback riding. Even Superman had an accident and some could be so severe. She would think we shouldn't be doing this, we are not horse people, and we were not raised around this. The family would mostly ride when their instructor was present. A few times Patrick, Elise and Erika along with mom would give her a bath, groom and love her. Rounding the corner to the pasture all would roll down the windows and shout out to Cindy. Cindy would look up and at them and they claimed her and felt bonded.

Seven months later Michelle would get a call from Duane that Cindy was down on her belly, and would not get up. Duane informed Michelle he had seen this before, *she was foundering*, he thought, and he told them to come out. The vet was called and it was decided to try and get her to the barn and rest for the night. They succeeded at this and over the course of three weeks kept her in the barn on a special diet and rest. She improved and was able to leave the barn but forewarned by the vet, this could happen again and be worse. This news was hard to digest but a decision had to be made and Duane found a place for Cindy to go to. It was hard for the family to give up on Cindy; but it was also a lot of work and time.

"Momma, you had your horse and now it's time for her to go; she's not for riding and Duane has found a home for her," James told Michelle. They would certainly miss Cindy and the farm.

Danielle was busy making the plans for the wedding and she asked Michelle to help her with the venue for the wedding and reception. Opting for a vineyard, they made the trek to North Georgia and visited the Three Sisters Vineyard.

"Beautiful vistas, this is absolutely gorgeous, I'm jealous!" exclaimed Michelle. Both agreed. "I wish I could do it all over again, it would be right here. Maybe my daughters will get married up here someday." They discussed music, food, cost and all the traditions in a wedding and a reception. The remoteness of the place was exquisite, yet challenging. So many decisions for Danielle to make in a very short time, for the wedding was to be July seventh two thousand and seven, or 7/7/7, (yes triple sevens).

Danielle and John made the decision in the end that the wedding would take place in Mexico. The Moon Palace, in Riviera Mayan, was an all-inclusive place. He was a bit worried after hearing so many stories of Montezuma's Revenge, while everyone tried to tell him that it doesn't happen anymore.

This was to be a family affair when Danielle asked Michelle to be matron of honor and John asked James to be his best man. The girls, Elise and Erika would be flower girls and Patrick would be the ring bearer. Even Grandma and Grandpa would be there!

Chapter Twenty

THE FISHING TRIP

John called his kids on his cell before he left the drive and caught up with them, telling them about his fishing trip and when he would return.

"Bye Dad, have a good time on the trip," Lindsay said ready to hang up.

"Hey, let me talk to your brother. Put Tyler on the phone, okay. See you next week when I get back," John said waiting for Tyler.

"Dad, what's up?" questioned Tyler.

"Hey. How ya doin? Just wanted to wish you good luck on the basketball tournament in Charlotte. Are you ready for it? Feeling strong? The knee, is it better?" John put all the questions, out there.

"Yes Dad. I'm as ready as I'll ever be. The knee is way better, all healed up, no problem." He continued. "The teams from North and South Carolina are really good, but our coach says we can beat them. Are you going to bring back some fish to eat?"

"You bet. Sure hope so anyway. I'll make a package for you as I know you love a fish fry. Maybe your Mom can make it for you, if not we can fry it over here," John added.

"Ok, great. Bye, Dad," Tyler said.

"Bye now," John hung up.

John had readied all the supplies and gear, and packed his Chevy Silverado truck last night. A small navy cooler was the only thing left to pack. He'd made a couple of sandwiches last night, and put some tuna, crackers and grapes in there a long with a couple of waters. He reflected upon last night with Danielle. Sitting on the couch and watching the television, she'd asked him where he was going. He'd told her Steinhatchee, Florida, which was South of Tallahassee in the swamp waters of the West coast. It would take them about five hours or so.

She'd questioned him about the swamp land and why on earth John would want to go there. We'll be fishing in the Gulf just north of the Suwannee River, called Deadman Bay, he'd said. She gave him the most dreadful look he's ever seen on her face. Her eyebrows got raised and her lips pursed, clicked her tongue and then she smiled. He could tell she did not know what to make of that area called Deadman Bay.

John had continued, rambling on with "Don't worry there's no babes in town, the best looking female has no teeth."

To which Danielle had laughingly replied, "That's too much information."

"Bye sweetie!" John smiled, jumped in the truck and for a second thought *maybe he shouldn't be going, after all, even though he took this trip every year for as long as he could remember.* Danielle just got here. He felt a momentary twinge of guilt, which quickly faded when she bid him goodbye with a kiss and quickly shut his door. She would be all alone at the house, and this might be difficult for her since there would be no phone service once he got into town.

He waved and turned on the radio. He was off to pick up the guys, his friend Doug was his age with a wife and kids, Duane, who lived behind him, a longtime friend who sometimes gave him guidance like a father, and Tom, an old friend of Duane's who was about 80 years of age. They were meeting at Duane's so they could park their cars or trucks and ride with John. It was a sunny day so the driving would be smooth and easy. This would give them a chance to catch up with all their lives and maybe any recent fishing stories to be shared.

Riding down I-75 with Duane sitting in the front, windows rolled partly down, and a little Stevie Ray Vaughn playing on the radio, John was in heaven. He liked that feel of friendship knowing someone, forever, who believed in you, trusted you and helped you whenever they could. How does that happen he wondered? How does someone care about you and you didn't ask for it, they just do? To him it seemed like that was even better than blood ties, a bond which asks no questions, just is. He liked it and he thought it would be there forever. He guessed the real question was could he and Danielle last forever? He smiled and said a prayer to himself.

"Give ya a penny for yer thoughts, my boy?" Duane said knowing he caught him thinking about Danielle. "I know what yer thinkin of!" Duane cocked his eyebrows up and down.

"I hope I found the real deal, man, pretty sure I did." John turned his head and looked out the window. "She makes me feel alive again! Except for you guys, because ya'll are the best and this trip; well, I'm never giving up this trip, ever."

"Getting married again are ya son?" Old man Tom hollered from the back seat. Chuckling he added, "Yep a true Southerner, just keeps on a trying til he gets it right."

"Oh, don't cha all worry now; I'll make sure he gets this one right. I'll pack her bags up and send her home if un ya all don't make it work right to yer satisfaction." Under his breath he added "and ta mine."

"I'm hungry, will ya pass me my sandwich from the cooler, a water too?" John said. They all ate their lunch while John continued to drive making the turn off of I-75 heading for the town of Live Oak. The scenery really stepped up and as far as the eyes could see there were rolling hills of green pastures, enormous live oak trees which seemed to extend their branches out forever, gracefully dipping almost touching the land. Looking closely one could see the Spanish moss gently hanging and swaying to the soft breezes. Brian felt this is how it must have been back in the civil war and most of these trees were here then, he recollected. He knew they were not in the Ocala horse country, but there was a few dairy farms. Twenty miles to go and they'd cross over the Suwannee River. The swamp would be all around them.

"This here road we're on, is it highway 51?" Doug questioned. Relieved to find out it was he added, "How about we get some BBQ in Cooks Hammock? Remember how good that was last year?"

"You mean the gator Q?" John couldn't help himself. They all burst out laughing. "Well it's 3:30 and we'll be there in about thirty minutes, so that sounds like a plan."

Pulling in on the dirt path which led to the parking lot John slid his silver truck into one of the three spaces left. "Here we are. He's open." John nodded to the other car.

Stepping back in time this place could pass for a 1930s boarded up shack. There was no paint left on the wood and quite a few pieces of wood had been nailed up replacing those that had fallen. The screen door with its wooden frame was slightly ajar and showed several small tears. The sign out front above the door was still in place and simply said *Teddy's Place* with red letters. Once out of the truck, the guys heard music *where skies are so blue.* 'Sweet Home. Alabama' by Lynryd Skynryd drifted out the screens from the juke box inside. Duane opened the door and asked, "Anybody home?"

"Hell yes, come on in! Been waitin' on you." Teddy beamed behind the small homemade bar. "You need some beers and BBQ boys?"

"Man smells gooood in here! That's what I'm talking about!" John looked around. There inside, the place was well kept, almost immaculate. The floors were wood and shiny, the walls were painted and adorned with framed fishing pictures of customers. Fresh washed curtains hung on the windows. Teddy had a brand-new juke box. He told them the distributors of his beer brought it here for him. I make money off of that there record player he joked. The guys could smell the BBQ and it smelled great. First up he doled out some Sweetwater 420 on tap telling them he just got that from Atlanta, won some kind of contest he'd heard.

One wondered, how did he make any money out here in the middle of nowhere with three parking spaces, two tables and five barstools. He told them many a dudes just take my Q to go, beer too. He said he didn't need too much money; they had expanded the road and the DOT paid him loads for the property that took his parking spaces. He'd kept the pool table, even though no one played much anymore. Three rooms is what he had, the bar and kitchen, the sitting area and bathroom, and the upper loft where he slept. He kept his boat out back on a trailer attached to his truck ready to roll out and go fishing whenever he felt like it. "Lord I'm coming home to you" he belted out and went to check on the BBQ and get the guys another beer.

John looked around the joint and glanced out the back window, and saw the hammock tied up between the two trees. It looked as though it got plenty of use, probably from Teddy here. He noticed an old book *Wind from the Carolinas* laying there on the hammock, and thought Teddy's life here was pretty simple indeed. His wife and child must be running errands today cause he hadn't seen them yet.

"All right boys, it's ready if you are." Teddy brought out four platters of pork, slaw, red beans and a biscuit; something new his wife was trying out. He served the BBQ sauce on the side which Teddy made himself every Wednesday night. He made several kinds, but what he found was the best was the vinegar-pepper type, a simple blend of hot red peppers that he grew out back and apple cider vinegar; he made that too, but bought the apples in Live Oak.

The guys were ready and beginning to salivate from the pleasant aroma coming from their food. Three of them watched as Duane put slaw on top of his meat and then he drizzled the sauce. "I might just try that, ah, that would be next time," John said and took a mouthwatering bite. Much later heading out the door they thanked Teddy, the proprietor, and said they'd see him next time or maybe send him a picture with their catches. He waved, bid them riddance and said

"Don't let the gators bite you."

John gave a quick call to Danielle, not quite sure when his signal would be out of reach, letting her know, so far so good. They would be there in an hour or so.

They were now in Dixie County and it was deep swamp land; everything but the road had water including the trees in the water. John wondered if any alligators might happen upon the road; did they cross the road like deer did at night? They arrived at the cabin and unloaded their suitcases, coolers and gear. Inside was just like last year, a set of bunks and two single beds, toilet, microwave, small burner, kitchen table for two, a light and a clock. Period. Rustic, is how Danielle might describe this place and then he laughed knowing she wouldn't set foot in here. It took about thirty minutes to unpack, and then they went to bed as fishermen do.

Up way before the crack of dawn, they loaded up the fishing gear and headed to the local marina, called The Sea Hag Marina, on Riverside Dr., on the Steinhatchee River. The time was about three thirty in the morning and they needed to rent a boat, purchase licenses, bait and snacks, too. A nineteen foot Carolina skiff was available; which they rented for the week. The guys filled out the forms for licenses, picked out some snacks and sandwiches, and decided on squid only as they had their lures and pop n plugs.

Leaving the dock old man Tom started in on the wisdom of fishing and they let him give this speel every year. *Maybe John would get something new out of it after all there is wisdom with age,* he thought. Tom started in on the Sun, the Moon, and the cycles of fishing with the tides. The fish feed with these cycles, at least they should, he explained. He went on to say fishing should be for pleasure, for sport, and there's no such thing as a bad day of fishing. He didn't believe in all these fishing gadgets and sonars, etc. They spent a couple hours in some of the low lands and then headed out to sea for some Redfish or Vermilion Snapper. This type of fish was very popular in the Gulf and fairly easy to catch, right off the bottom.

John pulled out his Slammer 360 with a gold and black Penn Reel. "Is that the rod and reel you got yourself for Christmas last year?" asked Duane.

"It is. It's nice isn't it? Let's see if it will do the job today?" John put forth and proceeded to put the artificial grub on, which was shrimp or new penny in color. He was hoping to catch few speckled sea trout, while they were out here. "Trout would be good but a King Mackerel or Lady Fish wouldn't hurt either."

"My wife wants redfish, the Vermilion Snapper, and lots of them. What's the limit now? Ten?" Doug asked. "She loves to fry 'em up, says they're the best tasting of all. I tend to agree."

After a full day, the first day, at around one o'clock or two they called it a day and headed in. Each had caught under the limit and all of them said a regular day of fishing, if there is such a thing. Not great, but not bad!

At the Sea Hag Marina they had their fish gutted, cleaned, packed and stored in ice in the largest cooler they brought. "Thought you told Danielle the best looking woman down here has no teeth," Doug said and eyed a woman over behind the counter chopping heads and tails off the fish. "Ha. Ha. Boy, were you wrong."

John looked over at the woman and smiled to his friend; both agreeing she had to be the best-looking woman he had ever seen in his entire life, except of course for Danielle.

"Hell, she must be new here since last year." John chuckled.

After two days of fishing and eating some of their catch, no showers, no television, no cell phones and no women, the men were feeling in sync, a coexistence with each other, which was working rather well. Tomorrow was the last day for fishing and then they would head home.

Climbing out of bed this last day they would spend at sea, down here in the beautiful gulf, the sunny light peering through the one window up front next to the door, John wanted to enjoy and remember it all. So he pulled out his camera and thought today is going to be a picture day, pictures taken by him to show Danielle what this trip is all about. He would end up taking pictures of his special tackle box Duane had bought for him probably ten years ago when his kids were little. He snapped up pics of his rod and reel, the boat and his buddies, the marina, the ocean and the beach and of course the fish!

Doug was testing out some lures and gave John some. These were the Cajun Thunder, a hot pink bobber with three beads when it hits the water it goes "cha-cha-cha," he recalled.

John tried it out throwing the lure out and made it dance on the water. "Cool with the shiny big minnow on the end, we are winning big out there today!" said John excitedly. "Let's go."

Today they decided to go way out and skip the river fishing or lowlands completely. Once out about ten miles they used the Cajun Thunder bobbers. Right away the fish were biting like no other day. As soon as they put their line down, a pull, a tug and sure enough a Vermilion Snapper, Mackerel or Lady Fish was on the line. Not even enough time to get the fish off the line and into some water; they just dropped them on the bottom of the boat and baited the line and dropped it in again. This was exhilarating and Tom, the old man, had to stop and sit and look around and gave out a big laugh and shook his head. "Unbelievable, absolutely unbelievable, in all my life, I swear this has never happened to me."

"What do ya reckin there, old man? Ye got an answer fer that?" Quizzed Duane.

"Yes, yes I do. Not enough fishermen in these here gulf waters." Tom smiled. John was having the time of his life, but he figured he best put some of the fish in some water or there would be no place to step. He cleaned up the bottom and rejoined as fast as he could. This fishing frenzy carried on for what seemed like four hours, though actually lasting five. Since they were catching all types, they had not filled the quota or limit.

Tom passed out some drinks as he had to stop to rest. When John stopped to have a drink and look out over the sea, he noticed the dark sky over land and turned on the radio. "Hey guys look over yonder, a storm brewing, probably should head in. He turned on the radio which they had not used as the weather had been great all week. He calculated that it might take an hour to get in and was not sure which way those dark clouds were headed. Slowly, he noticed a slight change in the direction of the water, very subtle.

"Small craft warning advisory for Deadmans Bay and surrounding areas, until three PM." The lady on the radio announced.

John noticed his line tugging and reeled it in, a long trout was at the end. With that he said, "We are out of here." Soon after the shore line was gone. Doug looked for the life jackets and couldn't find any. John noticed the compass wasn't working either. It was definitely a wet ride in, as the wind was offshore and spilled right into the boat. The worst was at about thirty minutes in, John had to slow the craft as the grey waves broke with white caps all around.

The rain came pounding down, too. Where did this come from, this fast and furious storm? John took a deep breath and said a big prayer. "God help us!"

"Cha-cha-cha!" Duane looked at John and said, "It's all gonna be all right, just know that son," Duane smiled.

John stood and handled the boat with steady hands and patience, and inside felt if Duane said we were going to be all right, then so be it. We were. The waves lessened after another twenty minutes, but the rain continued hard. Soon John spotted land and the opening to the river, the Steinhatchee. He looked over at old man Tom, his face strong and not even a worried look. What was with these men, guess they've been out here before in bad weather. Doug over there looked like he'd seen ten ghosts, in fact he almost looked sick like he was going to puke.

"Oh! My! Gosh. He's getting sick. Doug, do it over board man," John yelled out. Duane helped him to the side as John slowed the boat down. "Oh, God, help me, I can't look."

Ten minutes later when they began nearing the beach area north of the entrance to the river, they spotted activity with a bunch of people. "Looks like there setting up a party, a beach party or something," John said.

Exhausted by this day, they turned in the boat, loaded up the fish to be cleaned and headed into the Sea Hag Marina where they were greeted by the gal from the other day. Greetings and exchanges led to what was happening on the beach. She said they were shooting a swimsuit calendar for The Sand Times, and as soon as she finished here she was going to be in it. She was fileting a few of the largest fish caught. The guys stood there and watched her as she really knew what she was doing; like she had been doing this a long time. She was quick with the knife and swift in her actions, slicing the head, tails and fins off, keeping the flesh and separating the bones off the backside. "Any of you catch a big one today?" Sienna inquired.

"As a matter of fact, I think this trout might be greater than twenty inches." John proudly produced his catch. He read her name tag, "Sienna, you sure know how to filet those fish, and so precise with the blade." He complimented her skills.

"Thank you. I've been doing this since I was a kid here at my dad's store. We throw most of the catch in the automatic cleaner, but the longest and largest we like to do by hand," she added.

"So are you in the photo shoot on the beach? What month are you?" John asked.

"I'm doing the surfing segment, I believe it's May! Can't wait!" She said excitedly.

John smiled and said, "Good luck." He must remember to get a Sand Times calendar, sometime. Tomorrow the trip would be over, too bad; but he was excited to see Danielle.

Chapter Twenty One

ENGAGEMENT PARTY

The decision to host an engagement party for her dear sister and fiancé was made in a blink of the eye. Mother joined in and said she help with the financial end; so to make it easier on all they had it catered by Cincos, a Southwest restaurant with an upscale flair. Michelle and James's finished basement, with the mahogany bar and bricked side patio, would serve as the setting and the Southwest theme in the basement only added to the fun. Once all the details were sorted out, they realized this was becoming like a post wedding party or a reception. This actually delighted everyone as there would be no big party following the wedding in Mexico, only family was attending that. Danielle selected invitations and Michelle picked out cakes from Publix, a small chocolate round bachelor or grooms cake with a single large strawberry on top.

The second cake was to feed the crowd and had celebratory words on top. Michelle and John registered for gifts at two retailers; friends and family could purchase gifts they needed or desired. Michelle and Michael invited their close friends; those who knew Danielle from her living here years ago, from being on the bowling league and other social gatherings. Danielle and Michelle's other siblings Kay, the oldest in the family, Jack and Jess, the twins and youngest were coming with Mom and Dad for this special occasion. How sweet that everyone could make it. Kay, single and a nurse in Ohio, worked in a nursing home. Jess was a writer and designing his home up north in Wisconsin, while twin brother Jack owned and operated a small energy power company. He held a new patent for placement of panels on buildings. They arrived a couple days prior to the event.

Michelle and Danielle shared a long phone conversation the day before the engagement party, most of it about the details and excitement surrounding the event. Her husband needed to have major surgery and it would be difficult. When a person is a healthcare worker, you know all too well the realities of what can go right and what can go wrong. She was going to try everything to keep it together, but it was difficult. Time would heal she told her and Danielle believed her sister cause she always fixed everything, she fixed people, she took care of her kids, house, etc. She always had it together, so Michelle would fix this too. Michelle thanked her for listening, she felt better and moved on to what she needed to do next for the party.

Guests arrived at about 6:00 pm and began commenting on Danielle and John, and how wonderful the story of how they met on Marta, the train which goes to Atlanta. No one could believe the tale. The guests just thought it the cutest thing that they'd heard in a long time. The fact that both of them were over the age of forty five and fell madly in love, further enhanced the already sated love story. Many were catching up or listening to the retelling of events and enjoying appetizers and spirits when Michelle announced it was time to toast!

"He likes to fish and he got a good catch. Both got the prize I'd say," Dad said. All eyes were on him now after the first remarks. He added, "They'll find out later they both got **HOOKED!**" Amidst the laughter, Dad smiled and said, "We are very happy to have him in the family."

Duane was next and rather subdued. However, he eloquently stated, "I am blessed to have John in my life and now, Danielle, is the best thing that could have happened for the both of them. A long time ago John and I drew on a napkin plans to build his house, and I have never been more proud than when we did that. We built his house, and now his house will be a home once again. Cheers!"

Lots of oohs and aahs were heard by the clinking of glasses for this occasion. Michelle was guessing at what came next was not rehearsed, but rather felt, a true genuine vocal expression. John stepped up behind the bar and spoke aloud. "Hey everybody, I want to thank you for coming, but I must tell you a little story and it goes like this." Everyone became very quiet and came closer to hear this.

"Danielle doesn't know this, but about three weeks before we met, I was at my neighbors on a Friday afternoon in the driveway." He looked for Brittany and Keith and met their eyes and smiled. "I told Brittany that I would just like to meet someone and have someone in my life, to share my life with. My roommate is fine but I'm ready to move on, to share life again. My ex has gotten married and got a new house. You know, I built this house for a family from the ground up and she moved out with the kids and now it just doesn't feel right. *My dream is still there just a change in the plan.* It feels so empty!"

He continued. "Three weeks later, I met Danielle on the train, and I wasn't even going to take that train. I begged my boss not to send me on that early train on Sunday morning; but he would not let me out of it."

John was shaking his head and finished with "I believe it was fate, because I was not going to go on that train. I have my boss to thank!" He laughed and spoke saluting, "To Danielle!"

Guests shouted comments out like *'to fate'* and *'to love'* and everyone joined their glasses in this toast with John's magical moment. The feeling in the air at this moment was that two people found each other so beautifully and that love does exist. There is hope for everyone.

Danielle had waited a long time!

Chapter Twenty Two

RIVIERA MAYA, MEXICO

Arrival at the Moon Palace was extraordinary, as the passage through the glass doors into the skyscraper size entryway, was nothing less than exceptional. The vast inside, largesse and colorful, exploded with mosaic tiles of all sizes; fresh floral arrangements seized your sense of wonderment bringing joy to your face, as your vision perused molecules in all directions. It is still so glorious! They headed for the counter to get in line for the check in. While there, Grandma and Grandpa spotted them and headed over. Danielle and John were with them waving, smiling, and coming right over to them.

Grandma looked like she had just won the lottery, smiling and clutching her drink with an umbrella in it. They were in bathing suits and smelled of coconut suntan lotion.

"You all have some catching up to do," Grandpa informed James. "Oh Patrick, you and the girls are going to love the pools; they go on forever."

"That's what I'm talkin about," John chided in. "Wait til you see the place … absolute … awesome sauce!"

Grandma Audrey suggested, "Meet us down by the pool as we've got some chairs saved for you. You can use your cell phone, too; because they work here."

"Okay, we'll get our luggage to the room and see you poolside shortly," James said handing out the room card to Michelle. "Let's get going."

Sauntering back outside, the five of them looked around for the golf cart line to be taken to their room. The air was heavily laden with the smell of floral aromas and a few perfumed guests. Michelle took in the occasional cigarette smoke, lingering; it reminded her of days dragging away, like you had not a care. These wafts did not offend her as she'd still be smoking if it wasn't so harmful; but that was a long time ago. Everywhere she looked, she was looking at color, if it wasn't green and palm like, it was peach, fuchsia or yellow. The off-white trim stucco on the buildings was soft and pretty, and the white pillars were clean and crisp. The sky was medium blue with sheets of white clouds billowing in the air above them, and the sea was neon-aquamarine colored; which required sunglasses to view due to the brightness. The golf cart quickly took them away along the paved trail in between hedges and vacation villas with the driver pointing out various locales for dining, swimming, ice machines and golf cart pick up spots, *not that they would need this thought* Michelle, but it was a good idea if one was wearing high heeled sandals.

Five of them in a room, well, she knew the day was coming that would require them to book two rooms. Michelle hoped that day was a long time away, but she knew better and it made her wonder if then they could go anywhere. Shake that thought and think about that later. Once inside the kids checked it all out, TV, ice bucket, jacuzzi tub right in the room with a swan towel, hammock out back on the porch, fridge with drinks, snacks and the bed. Hurriedly, they unpacked, put their swimsuits on, and together headed for the pool where the rest of the clan waited for them.

Danielle and John were enjoying this time in the pool with Grandma and Grandpa as this was their honeymoon also, a combination of wedding and honeymoon for the sweet couple. It was a vacation for the rest of us. Michelle could let Patrick, Elise and Erika go swimming all on their own as they were expert swimmers; however, she told them to check in every couple hours so she would know all was well. She found them hanging from below the bridge and jumping into the water with some other kids. This was definitely a kid friendly place with activities, either poolside or an activities center, in which they could spend half a day with noworries for the parents.

Michelle, Danielle and Mother planned the next couple days and figured out what interested who and when they could go. "Let the adventures begin!" Danielle sighed.

The adventurous ones being Grandpa, James, Michelle, Patrick, Erika and Elise decided upon the powerboat and snorkeling expedition. The small individual size powerboats held two persons each, so one adult, one child meant three boats for their party. Everyone seemed up for it and *how hard could it be*, thought Michelle? The guides passed out the life jackets and everyone assembled on the dock for further instruction. The main man in charge told them to follow in a straight line, all the way out to the ocean, as we were in a bay and had to go out under the bridge. You were to keep your eyes on the boat in front of you, don't worry about anyone else but yourself and the boat in front. The two guides, one in front and one at the end of the line, kept everyone else in line. The white boats were about twelve to fourteen feet in length with enough room for two people and that was it.

Miniature little speed boats thought Michelle "I think Danielle, John and Mom are missing out on this one." Grandpa looked at her and chuckled with raised eyebrows like he wasn't so sure. James and Patrick took the first boat, followed by Michelle and Erika. Grandpa and Elise were in the rear, followed by the guide boat. It was sunny and bright outside with barely a cloud in the sky. The water in the inlet was more azure like in color with the edges along the groves or shrubbery almost an indigo. One could see down a few feet into the water. But there was too much to do, Michelle realized, as she must take control of the boat and stay in line. The little power boats careened past the photographer and they were on their way.

Well, *this was the life* thought Michelle, *wind in my hair, on the water, one of my precious little children by my side and an adventure to boot*. Ear to ear smiles is what she saw when she looked at Erika sitting next to her. Michelle turned her head to look at Grandpa's boat behind her and to see if they were enjoying it as much as her. Grandpa looked happy while Elise looked somewhat dazed, possibly unsure. Michelle thought, *she had put the bravest of the twins with Grandpa,* since they both couldn't go with her. Hopefully, this was the case as she would not want any tears or anyone to be afraid. Grandpa was more than capable to drive a boat as he was a very active man who golfed, drove a car and was a very good swimmer. It was before lunch and no one was tired. They were going down what seemed to be a channel through the brush of groves, which happened to grow right out of the water. Wondering if there are any gators swimming around in there, Michelle reminded herself best not to say that out loud. John and Patrick's boat began to slow down, and the first guide boat had turned around and was heading past them. Just then she turned, and saw that Grandpa and Elise were not behind them anymore.

"Oh, no, where are they?" Michelle's eyes grew very large and she gave James a two palm's up in exasperation.

The guide boat told them to wait in idle, while he went to retrieve them. Ten minutes later, he returned, and told them to follow him back as Grandpa's boat was not working properly. It was not running and they were getting him and Elise a new boat! Erika and her mother exchanged worried looks; however, this guide system thing seemed to be working.

The power boats, all filed in their singular line, were coming upon Grandpa's and Elise's boat. Idling up next to them, Elise started to tell us she saw a shark, and then it swam away. She went on to say that she was going to swim ashore cause she was scared when their boat stopped. Everyone was way out of site. She just didn't know what to do she said; but she insisted she saw a shark. Grandpa began explaining about his boat not working and soon enough they had brought out another. "Phew, let's get this show on the road!" He said rather loudly with a smile.

Now though, she must concentrate as they were off again and going full throttle. Michelle could see the open water right beyond the bridge and it was breathtaking! The light turquoise color was lit up almost neon, it was so bright and the full sun at high noon made it possible to look in every direction.

Out in the ocean, still single file with the shoreline getting further away, Michelle felt like she was in a James Bond movie or something out on the Riviera with boats chasing each other. All it needs is guns and maybe one of the boats to flip. This open water was exhilarating and handling the boat was all she could do as they were going full speed. She wondered when they would stop, she was ready to stop or slow down. She prayed Grandpa was handling things well, she snuck a quick peek and he seemed fine. In the middle of this experience, she remembered the horse ride in Jamaica, the wild ride she would never forget, it was in her top five all time adventures of her life. This would be added to that list.

They stopped as they had reached the snorkeling spot and the guides came around and dropped anchor. *It was time for everyone to go snorkeling.* You could see to the bottom it was so crystal clear. Michelle pushed the thought of sharks out of her mind, as they must not be anywhere near. They just couldn't be. Her kids were great swimmers. James, Grandpa and she could all swim well. Grandpa had been scuba diving a few years back and that was a big accomplishment!

The coral reef had so many colors and things growing on it. Fish of all sizes were swimming in schools, and an occasional crab could be seen. The brain coral was easy to point out and what an appropriate name for it. The sea was mesmerizing.

Chapter Twenty Three

THE NIGHT BEFORE

'Twas the night before the wedding, and preparations, most of them made over the phone by Danielle, would soon fan out in the course of twenty four hours. Tonight, would be a seaside dinner in an open-air restaurant along the boardwalk next to the beach. Floor to ceiling windows blocked the constant breeze from the ocean, allowing a spectacular view from every table. Music played overhead with that familiar calypso sound; putting one in a trance of sorts with ocean breezes, blue skies and cerveza!

"The feeling is surreal right now, Michelle. I'm getting married tomorrow; I can't believe it. I'm so ready. It feels like we are already married. John just loves it here; he wants to move here he says. Yeah right, a few more days and he'll be dying to get home." Danielle gushed, "I'm getting my hair done in the morning at the salon inside, nails too. Are you doing the girls hair?"

"Yes, I've brought special pearl hairpins to match their dresses and will pull it back simple like. I just can't believe this is happening! You are getting married after all this time and to such a nice guy. It's a miracle plain and simple. Everyone I tell your story to can't believe how you two met. I should write a book about this incredible and fateful beginning."

The party strolled down to the beach after dinner taking their shoes off to feel the sand, and check out what was happening. They found some comfy lounge couches to sit on at a beach bar and swings which, Patrick, quickly seized and set in motion.

"Watch out, your Mother will fall asleep and I ain't carrying her," Dad said. We all looked over at mother as she was sprawled out with her leg on Dad's lap. "Hmm. Totally relaxed. Now, how am I going to get her back to her room?"

"Well, Paul, you could throw some cold water on her or leave her here to sleep," James Thomas said with a smirk.

Elise said, "I'll tickle her feet!" And she did. This stirred Grandma and made her smile. She was relaxed to the max.

"What are they doing over there?" John asked the group. A large group had come down to the beach, and took over half of the bar then began passing about a large bong looking thing.

James looked and smelled a cherry scent. He checked it out and returned. "It's called a hookah. You smoke different flavors of tobacco with it. It's basically a bong. The guy said they were from California, where they have these hookah bars, and people go there to smoke flavored tobacco."

The scent wafting by did smell pretty good thought Michelle. "What will they think of next?" The night was dreamy all by itself with soft cool sand, gentle ocean breezes and visions of pure wedded bliss upon them. Hints of strawberry tobacco tickled your nose and smiles from sated tummies filled with seafood and drink, let one think that nothing could be finer at this moment.

"What's that?" James quickly sat up in bed.

"Oh no! It's Patrick, he's puking! Get up!"

"Honey! Oh dear!" Michelle scrambled but it was too late. Stomach contents were tossed everywhere. The girls got up quickly too, as they were all sleeping together. Mayhem abounded. The time, well it was four am. Poor Patrick, must have been something he ate they thought. James called maid service for a complete change of sheets, as even the bed skirt got hit. Back to sleep after a dreary eyed hour of cleanup. Thank goodness thought Michelle it was still dark out as she drifted back to sleep, and thinking the wedding was not until noon so they could sleep in a little.

"Momma! Momma, get up. It's time to get up, now!" exclaimed her little princess Erika.

"Are you sure? I'm still sleepy." Michelle smiled and thought today is here, yeah. "Somebody check the weather. I need a weather check." She knew this would get them running to the windows. She liked it when she thought of jobs to do and they took off like it was an exploration.

"Sunny out there, momma!" Elise shouted gleefully.

"Elise, you don't know, let me see." Patrick jumped in front pushing the girls aside. Because he was the oldest, he felt it his job to be the authority when mom asked for special reports. "Well, sunny, but I see two clouds, white clouds and the wind is not blowing," Patrick reported.

"Ok, it's a go. Let's get breakfast and come back to get dressed for the wedding," Michelle said.

"How are you Patrick? Feeling just a little better sweetie?" Michelle questioned.

"Mom, I'll be alright, I think," Patrick said in his best grown up nine year old voice.

John shifted in the king size bed and rolled over to his sleeping beauty. Hmm, did she ever look lovely this morning, looking at her sleeping with her hair so very soft laying all over the pillow. His thoughts wandered to just staying right here right next to her all day. He kissed her cheek to stir her just a little and her eyes remained closed but her slight smile gave him anticipation, frankly he didn't quite need right now. He looked over at the clock and yes, there was time. Rolling over and on top of his gorgeous bride to be he whispered, "This is the last time as singles, Ms. Danielle."

Grandma and Grandpa shared their early morning coffee. Rising up at breaking dawn Paul fixed the coffee, and served it to his bride of forty seven years. He started doing this when he retired twenty years ago as he could not sleep in, and it seemed like a way to start the day with Audrey. This pampering was their very own unique way of bonding after a life of work, children and time that passed by, too quickly.

"To Danielle and John, may they be as happy as we've been." Paul toasted Audrey with his coffee. "Cheers."

Audrey reflected, "I'm so happy for her that she found John, especially after a few of the heart brakes she endured. Sometimes, I feared she might never recover from those. But sweet John, well he's a rose in the garden. She's a lucky, lucky girl." Audrey's eyes welled and a single tear fell and this, this tear made her feel good.

Danielle sat up in bed quickly as she does everything in life, assessed the time, her clothes for the hair and nail appointment, her wedding dress, her jewelry, her breakfast and tea and put it all in order. She also had a special gift for John and she would put that in her purse and give it to him after the chapel service. She took a deep breath, exhaled and felt at peace.

She knew she was making the right decision by marrying him today. It all felt so right, not a bone or nerve in her body questioned this decision. She just wondered why it took so long in life to find this great guy. Had she not looked, was she not ready? She could not figure out these questions. Had her ship finally come in, and she was waiting at the dock looking in the right direction at the right boat? Whatever happened it seemed like a plan of sorts; like she could not have planned it better if she had tried. That was it, occurring to her right now at this moment hours before her wedding. A predetermined, destined to be situation, which her human hands did not have control over. She thought *I'm spiritual, I believe in God, but this this is divine and I am thankful. Destiny is within all of us,* she thought, waiting calmly, seeking you out catching you unaware, and helping you when least expected. Wow, she better share that with Michelle as she liked all that airwave, universe stuff. She smiled and lightly bit down on her lips and gave herself a, yes nod. Up now and … ready … set … go!

John ran into Michelle at breakfast and told her Danielle was at the salon. "Are you nervous?" Michelle questioned her brother-in-law to be.

"Who? Me? Uh … no. Not me. I've been down this road before,

taint nothing to it," jokingly quipped John, winking. "I know, I have found the right one for me, we have a trust and that is important. Period. I'm looking forward to it; today and tomorrow!"

"Great, I'm so thrilled you are joining our family," said Michelle. "See you later."

Chapter Twenty Four

SEASIDE WEDDING CEREMONY

The wedding was scheduled for high noon on 7.7.2007 in the seaside chapel, next to the beautiful Gulf of Mexico @ Moon Palace Resort of the Riviera Maya in Cancun, Mexico. The chapel was small and circular with windows floor to ceiling, allowing an opening at the top for air to circulate. Pews were on either side of a red-carpet walkway, with a simple stone granite alter between two large pillars closest to the beach. Three hundred- and sixty-degree extraordinary views, brought the entire tropical paradise into the chapel interior. An exquisite bridge with inlaid ceramic tiles over a small creek led to the entrance of the chapel. Palms dropped over from each side of this walkway lending the feeling of a languid stroll into fairytale land, appropriately placed for this storybook wedding. A constant warm breeze to blow upon the skin, and in effect a pretend cooling strategy from the Aztec gods, pre ceiling fans, was noted. The family party assembled as did the minister and wedding planner. Excitement was rising with anticipation and smiles on everyone's slightly nervous faces.

Michelle hoped Patrick would be okay after last night. He looked a bit pale that was for sure. Cameras were set and ready and all were situated in their spots. Moments were now few.

Grandma, James and Michelle walked to the front of the chapel and stood with John. He wore a simple white linen long-sleeved buttoned-down shirt, purchased by Danielle, with tan linen pants and teva sandals.

His tanned dark skin and hair was accentuated by the crisp white shirt. James wore a peach or coral colored Hawaiian shirt with tan linen pants and teva sandals. Michelle's dress was brown with a crème floral design, sleeveless and free flowing. A natural pearl necklace softened the neckline. Grandmother wore a soft Polynesian blue and lilac, free flowing silk, short sleeved dress with French grey small heeled shoes and a flimsy wide brimmed white crocheted hat. Real pearls accented her neckline. Danielle, Grandpa, Patrick and the girls were set outside beyond the bridge. The minister was set at the alter and nodded to the wedding planner.

The traditional Canon in D began with organ notes and violin pauses, this by Pachelbel, Danielle had chosen many moons ago and who wouldn't as it made your skin tingle. As Patrick approached the chapel wearing a light sky blue, cream, and floral Hawaiian shirt, not tucked in, with tan linen pants and flip flops, Michelle swallowed hard still not believing this day was happening.

She had just celebrated twenty-four years of wedded bliss herself. Enough. Enjoy. Patrick, her first born was all nine years of age, but fifteen to twenty in the making. He was her gift from God, his chosen name, wanted more than any child could ever be. A friend once told her you can never love them enough; she had been practicing this since his birth. That was her indulgence, love. He was a beautiful boy with thick blonde hair, blue eyes and full cheeks with tan Indian like skin. He could memorize a room and read books from an early age. He was smart and beyond; he just knew things! Patrick's eyes were so blue in that shirt, blue was his color! His face, though, looked pale, maybe even greyish. *Must keep her eye on him*, she thought.

The music continued and the girls, Erika and Elise, walked slowly side by side, *but not slow enough* thought Michelle. She could hardly look at both, she couldn't, must look at them separately one at a time and so she did. Elise was closest to her; sweetness only begins to describe earth and spice qualities in this child at eight years of age. Soft and composed, quick with wit, her tomboyish acts at times, belied her beauty and strength. Fast was her middle name, a runner. Erika to her left, an angel's voice, with kind words and acts centuries old, gave a knowing quality of inherent goodness. Tender and tearful, slow to anger, her girlish ways were pretty and powerful.

Michelle's throat tightened and seemed full, she smiled. Elise and Erika wore their first communion dresses; Strasburg designs which were timeless classics made as heirloom garments with hand embroidery, French seams and special stitching. Grandmother had purchased these last year for the church ceremony and they fit beautifully. The pretty flower girls had sleeveless 100 percent silk mid-length dresses, the color of magnolia petals, button down back with a wide tied bow. Sparkling gold and silver crossed slip-on sandals with slight heels bestowed their precious slender feet. Their soft light blonde straight hair was held back by pearl pins, three to each side giving off a cascading effect away from the face. They dropped azalea colored rose petals at intervals from tiny little white silk purses.

James and Michelle looked at each other when the kids had made it to the alter, and smiles of pure love and devotion emanated between them. Michelle glanced over at mother and she gave her a knowing nod of a Mother's approval and love. John looked handsome and slightly nervous with a small tight smile. The bride was up next!

The music switched to 'A Whiter Shade of Pale' by Procol Harum, an oldie but moving piece which James started whispering some of the words. Danielle and Dad were still outside doing whatever. "There is no reason, and the truth is plain to see….If music be the food of love, then laughter is it's queen…And likewise if behind is in front, then dirt in truth is clean …And so it was later, as the miller told his tale that her face, at first just ghostly, turned a whiter shade of pale……"

"You really remember your tunes; oh yeah, I forgot you spun tunes in college," Michelle metered out.

Michelle heard the music change again, and she turned around to see Danielle and Dad enter as the traditional wedding march began.

The bride entered onto the red carpet holding the left arm of her Father. Her day of glory and love was in front of her right here at her feet. Danielle radiated the glow from sun and a warmed heart all from love. Her fantastic features with striking dark brunette hair and a perfect smile with bright white teeth and curvy bodily features, shown like a goddess. This was her time to shine as Erika would say. They paused at the entrance and everyone snapped pictures. She was a beautiful bride!

Danielle and Dad began the walk on the red carpet, her dress a simple vintage gown, sweet like her had a crocheted upon lace chemise, silhouetted over the unique and charming mid-length silk taffeta thirties style afternoon dress. Her shoes were Italian like Cesare Paciotti ostrich leather, the elegant and stylish designer, multiple straps of silver overlapping to the center, which she bought at DSW. Her veil of white fell behind fluffed out slightly. Pearl earrings touched each lobe gently. Her hands carried eighteen azalea colored, perfectly trimmed roses. Stunning!

Dad wore a blue cotton shirt and tan linen pants with a brown belt and a closed gentleman smile. He looked like the proud and grateful patriarch of the family. No jokes now, just serious but pleasurable business at hand.

As the two of them passed by, tears welled in Michelle's eyes and she breathed a big sigh. About this time, Michelle noticed Patrick, leaning on the alter, moving from one foot to the other. She nudged James, and whispered, "Do you think he's getting dizzy?"

Patrick turned around and looked at his Mom. She nodded for him, to come and sit down, in fact lay down, if necessary. He set the pillow with the rings on the alter and stepped down, walking to the back of the chapel. James got up and checked on him, pale and somewhat green at the gills; he laid down and seemed to be ok. The ceremony continued……for now.

The minister did the usual affirmation in the beginning and added 1 Corinthians 13:4-7 about love.

L O V E

is patient.

is kind.

does not envy.

does not boast.

is not proud.

does not dishonor others.

is not self-seeking.

is not easily angered.

keeps no record of wrongs.

does not delight in evil.

rejoices with the truth.

always protects.

always trusts.

always hopes.

always perseveres.

Vows were being exchanged and signatures written in the Mexican book of marriages, when Danielle began to lean from one foot to the other. Pursing her lips together slightly, she took a deep breath and continued for a moment or two. Then that stretch of the neck a person does when they are checking themselves to make sure they can still stand occurred. This is when the minister nodded, looked at John and suggested Danielle retreat to the pews. John helped her to the first pew, where Grandma and Grandpa were sitting, by holding her arm and back as they walked. We all came around to check her out.

"She could be getting the same thing as Patrick," James offered up. Michelle sat down next to her and began feeling for her pulse, checking her eyes and talking with her, after all she was a nurse. She knew what to do.

"I can't feel my arms," Danielle faintly ushered out from her lips.

"Oh. My. Goodness, okay. Here's what we need to do. We need to lay you down because your blood pressure is probably nil. Girls, go get the napkin from breakfast this morning, it's at the cake table in the back and wet it in the ice bucket. Bring it to me right now, ok?! Mother, take your hat off and let's fan her. Raise her feet slightly to get some blood up to her head." Michelle quickly asserted.

"I'll call the front desk and have them send a medic," the minister offered.

It was stifling hot in the chapel; everybody was sweating and the bride, well, she probably had a good case of nerves. This heat was unbearable or maybe she was getting what Patrick had.

Michelle knew what she needed to do. Once we could get her blood pressure back up, we could walk her to the bridge, where the breeze would cool her down. The medic or lady with the bp cuff showed up, took her pressure and sure enough it was 82/50 laying down. That was low, but at least Danielle was healthy. Even so people could have strokes and where was a hospital out here? Michelle did not want to think of the terrible possibilities. So they cooled her down with a napkin of ice water, Michelle had learned this trick at the Red Cross tent at the Peachtree Road Race, when she worked it and sent runners to Grady. It ruined the front of Michelle's hairdo from the salon, but that was fixable!

There was the bride laid out on the first pew of the seaside chapel with all of her wedding Party; her family very concerned and anxious with Patrick laid out in the last pew. Oh my. What was she thinking having a seaside wedding in a closed chapel at *high noon*? We all began to shake our heads, once she began recovering. We got her out of there as soon as we could as it had turned into an oven! Sitting on the steps of the bridge she caught the hot windy air but it provided a relief and cooled her skin giving her some oxygen. Sitting down helped too!

After a fifteen minute spell or so the minister finished in about a minute and a half. The recessional tune was Beethoven Piano Concerto No. 5 E Flat Major Op.73: Rondo, an upbeat, fast and slow, on and on, loud and soft piano score; kind of like life. Exiting quickly, everyone threw the bird seed in their direction. John and Danielle went right to the cake and champagne table to cut the cake for pictures. Michelle would get the wrath for that later cause her hair was all messy. Michelle thought, *if she only knew how bad some of these situations could turn out; then she'd understand.* Now if this doesn't cut the cake, one sister faints on her honeymoon (Michelle) and the other faints at her own wedding (Danielle)!

Just outside the chapel under a tree the wedding party was arranged for pictures, and in the shade to the relief of all. In the distance the open air horse drawn carriage trotted around the courtyard gardens, winding its way to the chapel. The driver wore a large sombrero and fringed pants with a suited top and brass buttons. We escorted them to their waiting carriage and bid adieu. We all waved bye. "Where are they going now, momma?" Elise asked.

"Danielle and John are going for a little drive around the Moon Palace Plantation, dear." Michelle responded.

We celebrated at breakfast the next morning with a champagne toast, which also happened to be our last morning in paradise. The wedding party was feeling better, especially Patrick and Danielle. The newlyweds were staying on another day as were Grandma and Grandpa.

"It is time…for the toast and a dance!" Michelle raised her glass and pulled out her written toast to celebrate the new couple.

"Now it's time for us to dance, Danielle!" John pulled her out to the floor.

Epilogue

Somewhere between the 1st glance on the train, the 1st cell phone call, And the 1st visit to Ball Ground two souls found their mates. This has been called fate, destiny and even the Luck of the Irish, but we know it is forever their story of how they fell in love! Strong, sweet, funny and fast describe Danielle, who has been, My little Sister, and my best friend over the years. Some of our escapades have been riding in my black jeep, Listening to Cars, lifeguarding at Sawmill Creek, Boating on Lake Lanier, and riding horses at St. Simon's. The memories are endless, full of fun and adventure. And now my family: James, Patrick, Elise & Erika, Is so privileged, to have her back in Georgia. John is her handsome, honest, hardworking n forthright Outdoorsman. A Father to Lindsay and Tyler, he is the Fisherman of course but they both caught the catch of their lives! All this love is a wonderment to see like spring in the air, it makes us all want to fall in love again! We'll settle for a sweet tea with lemon or a cold beer, As we rock on the front porch at their beautiful log home. While John cooks chicken on the Green Egg and Dani plays music floating out the window. Welcome to the Yeager's at home in the South. We are thrilled to have John join our family!

To: Danielle & John Cheers!
Thank you for this honor,
Your sister,
Michelle

Hola !

Danielle And John were united in marriage on July 7, 2007 in a quaint Beachside chapel Moon Palace Resort in Riviera Maya, Mexico. The chosen site for the Tropical wedding overlooking the Gulf of Mexico and the romance all started with a chance meeting on the Atlanta airport shuttle train.....

"Danielle, the announcement is just perfect. Who are you going to send it to?" Michelle asked.

"Everyone grab a tea or lemonade. I'm going to send them to all the people who could not come to the party at your place, a few relatives and a few friends of Mom and Dad's," Danielle said, rocking on the front porch.

John and James were talking beer out back while John put some chicken on the Egg. "I just love that Great Lakes Brewery in Cleveland. I've got to get me some Christmas Ale this year, they only make it at Christmas time. Burning River is what we're drinking right now."

"Good stuff you found, John, I use to make my own, never as good as this," James added.

Life seemed like it didn't need to be any better than this.

The End

By Caroline Clemens

Chapter One

Brandon left the townhouse but not before he heard the television weather report. It was the first week of November 2004, and the weatherman said he was expecting the first snowfall to come over the next forty-eight hours. Brandon walked briskly on the pavement, quickly covering the ten blocks in the early morning hours to get to his job at his uncle's barbershop. Most of the people that hung out on the curbs, or sidewalks into the early morning hours were someplace by now. *They'd found what they were looking for,* he thought.

He was staying at his uncle's place, temporarily, as his parents had met with tragedy by way of the highway. They'd been hit head on by a tractor-trailer six months ago. His sister, Riley, was married, and would be having her fifth child sometime in January. He was now an uncle, four times over, at the very young age of twenty-five.

He'd done a tour over in Iraq in late 2003, right after the war started, when he'd signed up for the Army, but inside he knew it wasn't for him. He wanted to see people living their life, and growing old with lots of chances if one worked hard. That was probably why he enlisted in the first place. At least that is what he thought. He'd grown while in the Army by a couple of inches; maybe it was all the food. He stood six feet and was rather lanky. He had brown eyes and dark brown hair, which had a couple prominent waves. Pretty average is what he thought about himself, if and when he ever gave that a thought.

His uncle told him he had star-quality hair, and he should know, as he owned the barbershop. He'd cut the hair of famous people before they became famous or well known.

His uncle was a black man who'd married Brandon's Caucasian aunt twenty years his junior. And this is how Brandon came to be working and learning his uncle's trade. Now his parents were dead and this was what was left of his family. His parents left no money, nor did they own a house. They were renters who made a small income and never wanted anything more.

Brandon supposed he could go back into the army or sleep at a friend's place but his uncle's offer was just too good. He told him he could stay with him for free, and he'd teach him the business. He wanted to cut back hours to go traveling with his wife.

It was still dark when he arrived and the uncle-owner opened the door for him.

"Morning, Brandon. It's going to be a busy day, lots of big wigs in town. I'll do the cutting today, we'll train more next week, okay?" Sam said.

Brandon heard the familiar music in the background. It was his uncle's favorite CD and he played it at least twice a day. He told Brandon he'd cut some hair of famous people, and Brandon only surmised that they probably came from the Chicago area. He never did brag the names.

"Sure, sounds good. I saw that the boxes came yesterday. I can unload those for you," Brandon said, thoughtfully.

"You can make the coffee, keep up with the laundry and do a few manicures, too," said Sam.

"Yeah, sure thing. Do you want me to make you breakfast, today?"

"I bought us bagels with some new cream cheese, chipotle and cranberry cinnamon. Try both of them to see which one you like best."

Brandon liked working here as Sam often brought him breakfast, something he picked up along the way. He knew all the places. *He had friends all over town or so* he thought.

That was the last of any conversation as Saturday had one customer after the other.

"I'll see you next Saturday," Sam said and waved goodbye. Sam wanted Brandon to come in during the week and he said he would in the New Year. He needed time to research the papers for opportunities until he made a final decision about his life.

"Sounds great. Hey, one of these Saturdays I'll need that holiday cut," Brandon said, remembering Sam told him he'd learned a new style he wanted to try out on him.

Brandon's sister, Riley, strode down the avenue all dressed up for her last shopping trip in Chicago. She knew this was it. Josh was sitting for their four children as she and her friend went Christmas shopping and out to lunch. Thus far she'd had no complications from this final pregnancy. They had no extra money with four kids, but somehow, Josh, had given her three hundred dollars and she was going to spend it.

Bags in hand she told her friend, "Please, let's eat! I must feed this baby, like now," Riley said with insistence.

"Absolutely, I see your favorite restaurant right across the street, over there," said Jasmine. She knew her favorite because it was hers, too. They both loved cheesecake.

The friends crossed the street in downtown Chicago, the very heart of the city near the lake. They walked in and were seated. Immediately, they relaxed, talked and continued to enjoy this special day. They shared laughter and smiles and pictures of the families they had both made so far. There was much to talk about.

Her friend pulled out her cell phone and made a call to check on the family. Riley had no cell phone. That would be nice to call Josh, and check on the kids. She should put that on her wish list. Actually, she would be so tied down with kids and appointments and school, where would she find the time to do anything beyond have a cup of coffee in the morning? She knew this was her life and she liked it. She missed her mom and dad so much it pained her, but she barely had time to think about that, too.

Her friend handed her a couple of the pics they'd taken at the photo booth earlier. "These are for you."

"Thanks. Thanks again for coming today. You are a great friend," she said as her eyes teared up just a bit.

Two weeks later Brandon sat in the chair with the longest hair he'd ever worn in his life; he anticipated Sam's magical shears on this Saturday morning. When it was all over, he checked himself in the mirror. Well, he looked like Cesar. Yes, Julius Cesar.

"Are you sure, this is the cut? It is mighty short," Brandon questioned reluctantly.

"Yes, it is the thing, trust me. You look very handsome, I mean cool," Sam said and winked at his young prodigy. "Today will be slow as everyone is starting the holiday shopping. Just hang out, and we'll see what happens around here."

Brandon nodded, "Okay, I think I'll read some of your newspapers over there and have a cup of coffee."

Brandon perused the papers and checked out the headlines. He saw a print black and white newspaper from Wyoming. Why on earth did Sam have a paper from Wyoming? He leafed through it, and read this and that. He saw an ad, 'Help Wanted: Farm Workers, Ranch Hands, Migrant Workers and others to do year round work on a family owned ranch. Housing and food, some cash.'

He wrote down the phone number and decided that maybe he might call them. Would he actually go out and work on a ranch? Would they even say yes? He read further and it said: help needed immediately. Brandon took a deep breath followed by a long sigh.

That night at home he called them, and someone picked up the line. A man told him he needed five more people, and he thought *Brandon sounded perfect*. He told him he would buy him a train ticket for the day after Christmas. He would just have to show up, give his name and ride the train to Cheyenne. From there he would pick him up, and bring him to the ranch. The guy named Tracey gave him three references to call, so that he would know this was a legitimate job.

He felt pretty good about it, but just to be sure he would run it past Sam. Sam would know if it was to be okay; he just knew those things.

Brandon had made a decision, and it wasn't rocket science, a fabulous job or education, but it was work, a different kind of work. He would be around animals and farming, working for himself at something new. He would be getting away from this urban decay of sorts: the buildings in ruin, the people that hung on the streets, and the late after hour's folks with nothing to do.

The distant gunshots and stories that didn't make the front pages, anymore, bothered him more than he let on. He wanted to get away and try something else. He smiled as he took a cab to his sister's house on Christmas Eve.

In the morning he packed his bags, and thanked his uncle for letting him stay there. He'd be in touch but planned to be gone for a year, or two, and learn as much as he could about farming and ranching. Sam told him he could come back at any time, and resume learning the hair trade. He told him he would always have a place for him, as he was his wife's nephew and that was family.

His thoughts went to his sister's house last night. It was the smallest duplex in all of Chicago, but she kept it clean and neat. She had a very small, live tree which the kids had decorated. The buffet she put out lacked side dishes but it was full of love. She did her best with the free turkey someone had given her. She thanked Brandon for going to the store to buy a couple side dishes. He was glad he could help out. Her kids Cierra, Adele, Chloe, Alex and the one, not yet born, would be lucky because they'd have this great mother, who would always do her best with whatever she had. Always.

Riley's son, Alex, had his hands full with all the girls around him. Brandon would miss them, and probably, if he thought about it too long he shouldn't go. But he had to find out what he was capable of and he had to do it now.

Josh picked him up and drove him to the train station with the whole brood in the car the day after Christmas. Brandon swallowed hard. Man this just might be harder than he thought it would be. He looked back at his place and the snow on the ground. He would come back but he would be different; he just didn't know how or what.

He and his sister departed the car as Josh pulled away. He said he would come back in twenty minutes. He kept driving around to keep the younger ones quiet. Riley and Brandon walked arm in arm. He wanted to hold her up as she was in a delicate physical state.

"Oh, brother. I'm going to miss you!" She let it out.

"I will miss you, too!" he replied. "But think of all that we will do while we are apart. You should get a cell phone, and I should, too."

"Yes, but the monthly costs are so much. Maybe, I'll get one of those disposable ones," she said but lied, as she knew it would be a long time in getting any luxury.

"I'll write you a letter, and I will be coming back to visit. I promise," he said decisively.

She turned to look him in the eye and knew he was telling the truth. She could tell. She smiled happily. "I love you brother, come back when you're ready. Learn something you never knew and surprise us all."

Brandon loved his sister and decided he needed to tell her that now. "I love you, too, and all of your family. Thanks for everything and especially Christmas Eve. Maybe, someday, I can repay you, you know, give it back."

They both looked around at all the snow and knew it was time to say goodbye for good. The train whistled in the station, and Brandon turned to give his big sister a hug allowing room for the baby. She hugged him back slow and sweetly, and then let go. After all, they both, recently and tragically, had lost their parents. Riley looked over at the curb and saw Josh waiting for her.

"All the best to you, Brandon. Mom and Dad would be proud you are going out west, and exploring, maybe finding something new … something you never did, or they never did. Good luck," she said.

"I don't know it might be foolish," he said.

"Go ahead, be a cowboy. Send me pictures," she laughed.

"A cowboy, well, I hadn't thought about it like that. Cowboy, do they even exist?"

"They will now when Brandon arrives," she said, and laughed.

"Thanks and bye," he said and turned away to leave.

Brandon found his seat on the Amtrak train, and was settled when it departed Chicago for Cheyenne, Wyoming. He'd been to training for the Army in Texas but he'd never been anywhere else besides the south side of Chicago. He felt somewhat free at this moment, and he was not afraid. His sister on the other hand cried all the way home, and the kids heard her sobs. They felt bad for their mommy.

He drifted off to sleep and then later awoke. He periodically looked out the window. What he saw was the vastness of America as it went on forever and ever. He could hear the occasional Christmas tune after a passenger pulled his or her ear buds out.

"Where are you going?" the old lady with silver hair sitting next to him asked.

"Wyoming and you?" he managed to be courteous.

"Washington. Yes, I'm going all the way to Washington. My daughter lives in Seattle, and I've never been there. I hate to fly, so here I am on the train," she said.

Brandon didn't know if she wanted a reply, or what, so he managed to give her some big eyes and a nod.

"What does Wyoming have that Chicago doesn't have besides the obvious?" she asked.

"I'm going to find that out. It will be my first time there," he replied to the quick wit of this lady.

"I'm sure you will find more than grass and mountains. Have an adventure while you are there, cowboy," she said and smirked a bit.

He shook his head and looked out the window again. Next thing he knew she was gone.

The announcement came from an attendant that Cheyenne was

fifteen minutes away, and people departing should get prepared. He was ready. He looked out one last time, and the ground was white with a sky blue above in the heavens.

He didn't have to wait at the station as Tracey spotted him and came right up to greet him. "Brandon?"

"Yeah, that's me. Are you Tracey?" He inquired.

"Yes. Glad you made it. Where are your bags?"

"This is it," Brandon said and showed his bag.

Tracey viewed his new worker, his new ranch hand and smiled. He put his hand out to welcome him. "I'm glad you are here as I really need your help."

"Good. Can't wait to see the place," Brandon replied.

"Oh, you've been looking at it for the last twenty or thirty minutes from the train window," Tracey replied.

Brandon wasn't ready for that. "What?"

"Yeah, I own the ranch coming into town. There are so many acres I can't count them nor see all of them. Now you know why I need more help," Tracey said lightly as he spoke the truth.

Brandon got into the truck, and the two of them headed to the ranch. "It's cold but not too bad today, not as bad as it can get out here," Tracey told him.

Brandon felt fine. He knew he'd be okay, and began to feel glad that he came this far. He looked out the window and suddenly he felt small. Off in the distance he saw an old house with weathered wood, trim and boards. It looked in need of repair. It looked even worse than the homes in Chicago. *Nobody actually lived in that house*, he thought. But he saw smoke coming from the chimney, unbelievably, so he knew they did. He looked over at Tracey for a moment.

"That is one of the houses on the ranch that needs repair for sure. We'll get to that in the spring, I hope. There is so much to do, Brandon," Tracey explained.

A couple miles later, Tracey pulled onto one of the longest gravel drives Brandon had ever seen in his entire life. It must have been two miles or longer.

159

Caroline Clemens

<h1 style="text-align:center">Chapter Two</h1>

"Did you celebrate Christmas?" asked Tracey.

"We did. My sister, Riley, has the big family. Lots of kids and torn wrapping paper was everywhere. Chaotic actually," replied Brandon. He'd gone over Christmas Eve and celebrated with a party. He returned just after most of the presents were opened on Christmas Day. He'd spent the morning packing, getting ready for this trip.

Tracey replied, "Yes, I know the chaos as I have four little ones."

"So you had a Christmas celebration yourself, then?" Brandon asked being friendly.

Tracey just shook his head and smiled. He was born a Navajo in Arizona and had moved up here to Wyoming, where he met his wife, Keri. She was a Cheyenne and very beautiful. Her family had been in the sheepherding business forever. They were also farmers. The two of them worked hard on her family's property for years.

Unfortunately, her father's property had to be sold and it became a part of a national park. Her dad had given her and her brother the money from the sale, that's when she and her husband bought the ranch where they now live.

Family was everything for Keri, and her dad's gesture was not a surprise when he did this. He wants them to work hard and prosper, but he also realizes it's tough out there to get started. Tracey wasn't sure he could ever repay her dad, and to that he replied, "You don't have to. No one owns the land; we just borrow it and use it. Take good care of what you've been given."

Tracey was a quiet man with few words, hardworking to a fault but always there for his family, and his workers, as Brandon and others would soon find out. He truly cared and was given much.

He especially liked the horses in this business, and would soon expand the operations of this ranch with cattle. He would do that in the spring with the help of his new hands.

The truck pulled up to the house, and Tracey pointed out where he and his family lived. It was largely built of logs and held a solid stone porch out front with chairs for sitting. Four barns were situated out back of varying sizes: one was extremely large and probably held the tractors and such, another two were medium in size and the last one, which was the smallest, would be where he and the other ranch hands would live.

Brandon grabbed his pack and followed Tracey to the 'bunk house' as he called it. He showed him around, and told him after he was settled, in a few hours to come and join them for dinner at the main house. The bunkhouse held twelve inhabitants and was not full by any means. They had a television, couches, and a kitchen area, along with two showers and three toilets.

Brandon looked around and thought *this isn't so bad*. He unpacked his belongings, hanging some items and using a couple drawers for the rest. A couple of the other guys here introduced themselves, and invited him to go for a ride across some of the property. They'd be looking for any stray sheep or wild animals on the ranch. They said it would only be for an hour or so, as they were going up to the house for dinner, too. He joined them after they told him to bundle up as the wind gets mighty cold when going across the plains. Once he was outside, and climbing aboard the three-wheeler, he understood better about the wind being cold.

They traversed across the plains at high speeds, and Brandon held onto the driver, as he'd be instructed in a few days. *He could see for miles and miles, probably fifty to a hundred miles,* he thought. They passed by a very large corral of horses. His guide or driver told him the kind of horses they were. He said they were quarter horses and they worked the livestock. They were also good for sports like racing, jumping, and showing. He told him they were intelligent, too.

Already he was learning and seeing so many new things, he hadn't even been an hour off the train. Brandon, age 25, from the south side of Chicago, already knew he'd made a wise choice. He said a quiet prayer to himself, a thankful one.

One of the guys said aloud, "We won't be using these three-wheelers much longer when the snow gets thicker in a few weeks. We'll have to use the snowmobiles or horses."

The lights were on at the main house and the guys could see the smoke coming from the chimney. They'd have a fire tonight. Through the back window Christmas lights glowed adorning the family tree. Brandon wondered if Native Americans celebrated with a tree or what? Well, he could see the tree, so he supposed they did.

They all sat at a picnic style table with long benches on each side. He met Keri and she was beautiful like Tracey had said, kind, too. She served the guys and her family tonight all together. She said when the rest of the crew came aboard, her family would eat at the dining room table, and the guys and gals could have this room.

She'd made a beef stew with cornbread and gave them sopapillas with vanilla ice cream for dessert. Once the dinner was done, the kids came back with their prize from the holiday celebration. He learned their names and they were Aspen, Autumn, Montana and Tallulah. *How unique* he thought. He guessed they might need a Summer or Winter in there, maybe even a River. He smiled.

The young men retreated to the bunkhouse but not before thanking their hostess and boss.

The next morning the three young men made their way to the medium sized barns, and began showing Brandon the equipment and jobs to be done in the wintertime, mainly feeding the horses and livestock. They showed him the wall of cowboy hats and told him to pick one out. And so he did. Later, next month he would learn how to shear the sheep.

Week after week went by escalating into an extremely cold, snowy winter. He learned how to: keep warm, feed the horses, groom them, check their hooves, check for ticks, (usually a summer job), give yearly shots, dressing, riding, and of course the manure cleaning. He had to check fences, miles and miles of fences.

The horses were kept in at night, and out during the day, so this kind of set the pace, the daily routine. Brandon and the other two: got up at sunrise, ate breakfast, tidied up, went out to the barn, fed the horses, gave them water, and led them outside in the corral. Then they'd go out and check the sheep.

The boss had told him he was buying cattle in the spring. Fencing would be installed when the snow melted. There would be planting in the spring and the equipment for that was held down the road in very large barn. They shared this equipment with Keri's brother and several others. They checked the firewood piles and loaded up wood for their bunkhouse, the main house, too, as both had wood burning stoves used for heat.

The guys played cards and made good use of their off time. They read books, and occasionally, watched a movie. Usually, by nightfall their bodies were tired. The weekends were lighter as they did the majority of the work during the week. More help was coming in the spring, around April, Tracey told them. Then the place would be busy and going all day long.

One of the guys told Brandon, "When spring comes, we'll go to town and show you where we hang our hat and spend some summer evenings."

"Sounds good."

"Once you learn everything, we can take you in town. We don't have to wait until May," the oldest one said. "Maybe when you get a paycheck and some of the others show up."

Brandon nodded in agreement.

Brandon learned about the four grains grown on this vast 'empire' as he called it. Wheat, corn, oats, and barley were the big four. He might not work all the fields, but he was told he needed to know about all of them, in case there was a need. Tracey wanted his men and women workers to know all of it just like he did.

The guys told him there would be a window in the spring: after all was planted, fences made or mended, animals out to pasture, and gardens planted that they would get a week or two off, not completely, just much less to do until summer came. He was told to enjoy that. He smiled.

Brandon took a shower and dried off. He glanced in the little mirror which hung above the sink in their bunkhouse. He had made some muscles especially in his arms and chest. He noticed his face seemed more defined, that's when he noticed he needed a haircut.

The guys and gals were all headed into town today right after lunch. It was May and the fields had been planted and all major work was done for now. There would be plenty to do in about two to three weeks. "Enjoy," is what Carlos, the eldest hand said. Five more hands had come aboard, not the twelve Tracey wanted, but he did get some local help to fill in for the summer. Three more guys and two gals came. The three guys were migrant farm workers from Mexico with green card visas, and the gals were students from a small agricultural college. They were taking the summer off from course work to actually work a real ranch.

Carlos drove one truck and Rebecca drove the other. They all headed into town for lunch, the posse resembled a big family. Brandon was excited, as he'd only been to town twice before, once for lunch when he got his first paycheck and the other time for supplies. This was the first real break since arriving last December.

Once in town Brandon called his sister and checked on them. He wanted to hear her voice and know how the new little one was fairing. She told him the baby brother's name was Cheyenne, after Brandon's new town. He couldn't believe that. She was probably running out of names. He laughed. *What the heck,* he thought.

Brandon ate his lunch and enjoyed the company of the other hands.

Someone played the jukebox and a few others played darts. He just happened to glance out the window, which faced the street, when he saw her walk by. She stopped for a moment and looked through the glass. Did she see him? Were their eyes looking at each other? He remained frozen in time and didn't move. He only heard a whistle.

Frankly, Leia, was exhausted but no one could tell it. She'd just walked the four or five miles into town. She probably could have found a ride but she needed to clear her mind and exercise her body, her limbs. She never wanted to be like her, her own mother, who couldn't walk anymore.

Just before she made it to the store she stopped and was going to open her purse to get the grocery list out. She turned and looked into The Painted Pony instead, a bar on main-street where many locals and travelers ate lunch during the week. For a brief moment, she saw a man sitting there looking at her, someone she'd never seen before. He must be a ranch hand, somewhere, working out here in Wyoming.

She retrieved her list and went on to the grocery store. She would only get enough for two bags, as that was what she could carry. Yes, she decided she'd walk all the way back. That way she didn't have to be around her mother today. She just didn't want to have to deal with the demands again. Her aunt was there caring for her like she did every weekend, when Leia helped out at the main house doing inside work.

Leia Settles was twenty-three, half Native American, and lived with her mother. She took care of her mother after her dad-committed suicide. He'd lost the ranch they'd lived on their whole lives to the bank due to debt. She and her mother had been allowed to live in an old house on the property, mainly because of the generosity of the new owner. Leia worked in the main house on the weekends helping out the lady of the place. Sometimes she got to work with the horses, but lately, no because the boss had hired hands to help with ranching. The only time Leia got any time off was when her aunt came and took care of her mother on the weekends. She'd never been anywhere or done anything.

Obedient to her mother in every way, she really didn't wonder about anything. Today was like any other Saturday when aunt Lilly came and relieved her of her duties. Leia walked to town for the exercise and gained peace of mind by the time she returned.

She exited the store and turned right walking on the sidewalk with her two bags. Right in front of the bar she stopped, and turned her head to see if he was still sitting there amongst the people. He wasn't. That was good; she didn't give that a second thought.

She turned her head forward and began walking. She smiled and went on her way.

"Can I help you with those?" a voice asked her.

"No," she said immediately without looking.

"Please. I'd like to," he said.

She stopped, turned her head to the left, and stared into the biggest brown eyes she'd ever seen. How could she refuse?

"Are you sure?" she asked.

"Absolutely. Where are you going?" he asked.

"Out to the Settles Ranch. Do you know it?"

His eyes looked a bit confused but he said, "Do I know it? That's where I live at least temporarily."

"You must be one of the new hands Tracey hired. Are you?"

"Yes, but not real new. I've been here all winter learning the ropes," he replied.

She smiled and asked, "Where are you from?"

"Chicago," he answered.

"Chicago. That is a long way from home," she said but didn't really know.

"It's only a train ride away," Brandon said and suddenly wanted to know more about this girl. "What's your name? I'm Brandon."

"I'm Leia. It's nice to meet you, and thanks for carrying my grocery bags," she said. "I've never been on the train. Someday, I want to go see both oceans, but not in the same trip."

Leia walked along, and enjoyed talking with Brandon, the guy from Chicago learning to be a cowboy. She laughed out loud.

"What's so funny?"

"You."

"Me? Why is that?"

She stopped out in the middle of nowhere and turned to look at the young man. "You want to be a cowboy."

Chapter Three

The pair walked along the road which headed out of town, as they talked and shared some of their backgrounds. He filled her in about his family, or their lack of, and how his sister is all he has left, besides his uncle who's been so good to him. He told her about the time he went into the army and all went well, but he wanted to move on. He just wasn't sure. He didn't know what he wanted to be.

She listened then told him about her home and her dad and how tragic it was when he killed himself. She was devastated but soon took care of her mother fulltime, as they'd lost the ranch and any money. She didn't tell him that it was very hard; she left that part out. He was being so nice and she didn't want his pity.

As they walked along she thought she should point out some of the state flowers. "Look over there. Do you see that green plant next to the tumbleweed?"

He looked in her direction. "Yes, I see."

"That will be reddish with an orange tint this summer. It is our state flower the Indian Paint Brush, which is a wild flower. Sometimes, they call it prairie fire," she said.

"Prairie fire, well, I'll have to bring you a bouquet this summer full of prairie fire," he said and smiled.

She smiled back and said, "You can bring me the flowers, that's if you have any time off, cowboy. You do know that cowboys are extremely busy come June, and it continues until September."

"I've heard that. I will have to make the time."

The sound of a horn startled them. It was Carlos in the truck. He pulled over and shouted, "Do you need a ride?"

He asked her if she'd like a ride.

"Only if you do," she replied.

"Carlos, thank you. We're good. See you in a couple hours," Brandon replied.

The truck sped off with its riders headed to the Settles Ranch.

"Oh, we probably should have given him the groceries," Brandon said aloud.

"Please let me carry one. I insist," she demanded.

"If you don't mind. May I ask you a question?" he asked.

"Sure. What do you want to know?" she asked back.

"I know it's none of my business but why didn't you drive into town? Do you not have a car?" He asked and hoped it wasn't too rude.

"Sure you can ask that. After all you are helping me walk the groceries eight miles or so," she said and laughed.

He waited.

"I do have a car, well, it's not a car but an army jeep. It's broken right now. Also, it has no top. It broke down two days ago."

"Maybe I can look at it, maybe it's not serious. Possibly it's just out of gas," he said.

"Maybe, geez, hadn't thought of that," she quickly replied.

"You probably need something sturdier, durable, especially here in the winter time."

"My aunt Lilly is going to sell me her SUV at the end of summer. I'll be good. Thanks for thinking about that, though," Leia said in earnest.

He could see her house in the distance, man it still looked bad. He'd thought maybe the winter snows had distorted his view. No, it was in need of repair. Didn't Carlos say he was going to repair it in the spring?

Spring was here and almost gone now.

She knew he was looking at the house. She had lived in the main house when her family had owned the ranch, but that was then, and now, she didn't. "Hopefully, this house is temporary, sometimes I think it's going to blow over in the wind."

"No, I don't think that will happen. I think it needs some replacement boards and a little fortification for the porch," he said.

"Yes, I suppose. I've tried to fix up the interior but exteriors are not my thing," she said.

"Maybe some of the guys and I can come over before the summer rush and help it out just a bit," he said. "We could probably paint it, too, in a day."

"I'd make you dinner if you did that as I couldn't pay you. I'm sorry."

"That would be great, it's a deal," he said and meant every word.

They arrived at the front door and she politely said she'd take the bag, but he didn't seem to want to go. He didn't want to be impolite. He handed her the bag. She said thanks and went inside.

He said bye and waved.

Once inside she set the two bags on the small kitchen table. She looked out back, and her aunt Lilly had her mother out in the back yard. That was good for her, a little sunshine and fresh air.

She heard a knock on the front door and thought *who is here?* She went to the front and saw Brandon standing there.

She opened the door and he said, "I'm so sorry Leia, but I have another two miles to get to my place and."

She interrupted him and apologized profusely. "What was I thinking, please come in, let me get you something to drink."

"Thank you. I won't stay long at all."

She smiled. Thankfully her mom was out back.

"Maybe I should look at that jeep, you know, check the gas or something," he said with a polite smirk.

"Let me put away these groceries, and then you can check the gas," she replied sarcastically.

"Sure thing," he said. He looked out the back, "Is that your mother?"

"Yes, that's her and my Aunt," she replied.

"You didn't say she was in a wheelchair," he added.

"I didn't? I must have forgot. Three years ago the cane stopped supporting her, since then she's been in the chair."

"I'm sorry, for her and you. That must be difficult. Do you take care of her?"

"Since then, it's just me. My Aunt comes on the weekends, and I go to the store and run errands. I also go up to the main house and help Keri with her kids and stuff."

When she finished with the groceries she led him outside to the back barn to have a look at the jeep. The very small old building was about the size of a double car garage.

Her mother stopped them and hollered, "Leia, say hi to aunt Lilly. Who's that with you?"

She had hoped to avoid any interaction but that didn't happen. Reluctantly she led, Brandon, her new acquaintance over to meet her mother and aunt Lilly.

"Mom, this is, Brandon, he's going to look at the jeep for me."

"Brandon, this is my mom, Billie. And this is my Aunt, Lilly," Leia introduced all of them.

"Nice to meet you both. I'm going to take a look at the jeep if you don't mind," Brandon said. He shook their hands, and then waited for Leia to head back to the garage.

She excused them both and walked over to the garage. She opened the small wooden doors and led Brandon inside. There resided the once green army jeep, now slightly rusted and devoid of any color. She told him it started without a key, and he hopped inside and gave it a whirl.

After several tries he looked around at the gauges, especially the one that showed the gas level. For some reason it occurred to him maybe it was out of gas and the gauge was broken. That would be too simple. Surely, Leia, with her wits checked that out.

"Do you have any gas in the garage here?"

"Yes, of course. I keep some extra around, let me get the can," she said and sighed.

She handed him the can and she showed him where to put it. "Even though your gauge says half full, I think it might have broken, froze up-like."

He poured the gas in and left some in the can for future use. "I'll save you some, a little reserve."

He hopped back in and gave it a turn. It started. *He was lucky. In fact, this was his lucky day,* he thought all the way home to his bunkhouse.

$$\mathcal{C}hapter\ Four$$

*L*eia's mother, Billie, was taking more pain medicine lately prescribed by her doctor. Her severe arthritis which had partially crippled her hands and shoulders, had become prevalent in the joints of her lower extremities. It was difficult to move her into the bed at night, and get her back to the wheelchair in the morning. She seemed to be taking a turn for the worse, especially with the pain. Leia thought her weight might have dropped also.

"Leia, I need two more pills before you go to make lunch, honey," she told her daughter.

"Okay mom, but will you feel like eating? Maybe you should take them after lunch, and I'll put you down for a nap," Leia said like a true nurse would offer a patient.

"You're right, sweetie. Sounds good. Tracy called and said he's bringing a crew by to work on the house this afternoon and tomorrow. Maybe you should make them something to eat tomorrow after they finish."

"They are coming today and Saturday?" she questioned.

"Yes, you heard me the first time. I thought I'd get out of the way and stay at Lillie's tonight and tomorrow night. Will you be okay? Tracey's a good man, he'll make sure everything gets done right. He said you could borrow his truck if needed for your errands. I told him your new friend fixed the jeep," Leia's mother said.

"When is she picking you up?" Leia asked.

"She's coming at three o'clock. I have time for lunch and a nap," Billie stated.

"Okay, mom, let me put you to bed and give you your lunch in there. Then I can go get some snacks and drinks, especially if he is bringing a crew," quipped Leia.

"That will be fine. Lilly will probably come early like she always does," Billie said.

Leia put her mom to bed after she served her lunch which consisted of a sandwich and drink. She remembered the two additional pain pills prescribed for her increased pain in her hips and joints of the lower extremities.

Leia checked her wallet she didn't really have much cash. She decided to take some from the kitchen cookie jar fund as this was going to be a special day. Her little house was going to get some repairs at no cost to her or her mother. The best part of it all, of course, was that Brandon would be coming over. It had been two days since she had met the nicest young man all the way from Chicago.

She drove the jeep into town and picked up frozen lemonade, and a few lemons to give it some tang. She also bought a bag of pretzels and a container of nuts. She'd been to the bar and knew they always served pretzels, nuts and chips. Tomorrow she'd come back for the weekly groceries. That's when she noticed the guy across the street walking into the paint shop. It looked like Brandon. He must be buying the paint supplies for her house she supposed.

When she got home a crew was there replacing wooden ledges and boards around the windows and door. They were rebuilding the frames and making them more secure. They were quick, and seemingly, very skilled in this woodworking. She didn't see her new friend. He wasn't here.

She stayed out of the way and a few hours later Carlos came over to talk with her. "We will do the best we can Leia to make this a better place, more secure, less drafty in the winter time. But it won't be perfect, sooner or later, it will have to come down."

"Oh, Carlos, I know," she sighed. "You think it will last another year?"

"I just don't know. I just don't know," he said and shook his head.

"By the way, Brandon and two of the guys are coming over after dinner to set up for the painting tomorrow. At least the old place will look like new for the rest of the time you are here. You must think about where you will go, you and your mother. Maybe your Aunt has some room. You could come and stay at the main house but we don't have room for your mother, maybe she could be with your aunt. Do you think?" Carlos said, trying to figure something out for Leia.

She didn't like the conversation with Carlos. It forced her to think about what she needed to do. She needed to do something with her life. What about her mother? She was so young to be taking care of an invalid. She didn't know what to do. She really needed to talk with someone about this. Maybe she should talk with her Aunt.

In the meantime she put that aside as Brandon Smith from the Settles Ranch, her prior residence, was here to fix up her house. They would be painting it tomorrow. At least when it finally blew over or crumbled, which she hoped wasn't in the immediate future, her last days would remember a sweet little house and not a withered old shack. Yeah, she decided this tender loving care was a good thing.

She ran out the back door like she was ten years old and greeted her crew.

"Brandon," she said excitedly and beamed. He'd brought two others with him and they were all dressed in old clothes, ready to paint. She decided to join them and went inside to change. She was feeling like a kid without a care or worry. This was a nice feeling.

The crew, including Leia, worked until dark. They told her they'd be back first thing in the morning and the crew asked her to help them again on Saturday. She told them that sounded great.

Saturday was the perfect day to paint a house, even an old one. The four of them worked for hours and made this wretched old, haunted-looking house become, well, dare she say, a home. Temporarily she whispered to herself.

She asked aloud. "Should we paint the shed, the jeep shed?" She laughed.

"If we have the time, absolutely," responded one of the guys.

"How about red?" One of them asked. "We have a few gallons of it in the truck.

"Do you like it?" Brandon asked.

"I love it! I really do. Thank you so much!" Leia exclaimed.

She served the crew her lemonade and pretzels from the previous day when the work was done. After a while they decided it was time to go. She offered to make them dinner.

Brandon spoke to the other two who wanted to get going. They said, "Thanks anyway, we're headed back to relax in the bunkhouse."

Brandon turned and said to Leia, "How about you and I go to town to get your groceries, come back and make dinner together"

She smiled. That sounded like a plan.

Chapter Five

June in Wyoming was nice, not too hot, and cool at night when the sun went down. Leia was so thankful for the outside of her little home being fixed up she decided to work on the inside. Her aunt Lilly taught her how to use an old Singer sewing machine she found in an upstairs closet. She even brought her material she found on sale during one of her shopping excursions.

Leia taught herself to sew. With all the time she had to be there, for her mother, it worked out well. She could get up and down from the machine and work at her own pace. She wouldn't be seeing Brandon too much, as June would be busy as well as July on into September. She wondered if they would go to a rodeo, secretly she thought *about the two of them going to see a show.*

When she wasn't sewing and learning this new craft using her hands, she cleaned the place up and began painting. Carlos had dropped off more paint, interior paints and she selected colors for certain rooms. The place became brighter and the more she did the better she felt about everything. She even smiled at her mother and all she had to do for her. She had stopped wondering if it would always be like this and accepted that it would. Now that she knew her fate she only longed to spruce it up with color.

When she began painting the kitchen her thoughts occasionally drifted to the dinner she and Brandon made together after the outside painting. They had a great evening and played cards at the kitchen table late into the evening. When it came time to say goodnight, he told her he would be very busy the next month but he'd like to take her on a date this summer, if she would go with him.

She replied that it sounded like a wonderful idea, and she would be waiting for his call. He told her most likely it would be late June. "Can you wait until then?" he'd asked.

"Yes, work comes first. You have much to learn with the cattle coming soon."

"The boss said we'd have some time off, right before the fourth of July," he said.

"Great. You won't recognize this place as I'll be painting every room," she said proudly.

"You will be busy. I'll see you then before the fourth," he said and reached for her hands. He held them in his own. He thought about kissing her, he wanted to but didn't. He wanted their first date to be somewhere, and so he left her with his smile and warm eyes. She remembered it all. It was sweet.

She looked out the kitchen window and grazed her view to the garden which needed her attention. She would need to work on that today.

She turned the radio up and began painting in the kitchen, she'd selected the can that seemed pretty close to the color olive. That would go with the off white or cream colored cabinets and refrigerator. Although the refrigerator had been through all the inhabitants from the last fifty years, she surmised, it still worked. She wished she could paint that, too.

One last thought about Brandon had been about the horses. She was good at horses but it had been a while, three years since her dad lost the ranch and they had to move. He didn't like what had happened to him, and thought he'd let his family down after they had worked so hard for years. One night he sat in the kitchen chair, and she saw tears coming from both eyes. He dried them but she saw him swallow hard, and he had a distant look in his eyes. He wouldn't connect with her. She cleaned up, and he went outside to smoke a cigarette or so she believed.

About a half-hour later she, and her mother, heard the gunshot. He hadn't gone very far, he was just beyond the garage barn, near an old cottonwood tree. They found him sitting at the base slumped over.

It was just one more thing added to a list of problems that became almost insurmountable. They loved him and did not blame him for the sale of the ranch. He had worked so hard. It became his undoing. Her mother never spoke of him again. She clammed up. It was like he didn't exist, or hadn't ever existed.

Thankfully, her aunt gave her time to grieve and talk about him whenever she wanted. She looked forward to her visits every weekend. She would tell Brandon the rest of that story, when they were together, as she had left out some important parts.

She spent the next three weeks painting and cleaning, tending garden, and making some dresses for the summer. She made an extra one for her cousin who was about her size.

One day in mid-June Leia got a call from Carlos asking her if she could come, and help with the horses as all the cattle had come in. He could use an extra hand removing saddles and such. He said maybe just for a couple hours, as he knew she couldn't leave her mother for long at all. Leia said she'd like to help and she'd be right there. She put her mother to bed. She explained she needed to help Carlos out as he's been so good to them, and didn't have to do what he had done.

She took her jeep and quickly drove on the dirt road, the shortest distance to get to the Settles barns. She could see dust in the air for miles. It must be the new herd. She'd forgotten how many heads of cattle Carlos had purchased but knew it was big.

When she arrived the place was a flurry of activity. She headed for the barn, which held the horse supplies and started helping out. She removed saddles, washed down some horses, and put up the bridles. She also helped with the water, and dispensing hay and grain. There was plenty to be done with all the hands headed back out by the cattle pen.

She hadn't lost her touch as she had been around horses her whole life. She saw Brandon come in on Thunder, and he seemed strong, comfortable on her.

"Here ya go Leia. She's all yours," he said.

"She's a beauty isn't she? She's very strong. You are doing well to be riding her and with such ease. You are some cowboy now, huh?" Leia recognized his skills.

"You see me now, but you should have seen me a month ago. She bucked me, she did! I couldn't believe it but there I was butt on the ground and she reared her upper body. She showed me who was boss," Brandon said, giving Leia the full account.

"I'll clean her up, and give her some hay and water."

"Thanks. I've got to go and help with the cattle. Carlos got himself quite a herd, full of steer, cows and several bulls. He even has some baby cows. They are so cute!" Brandon said excitedly.

"Can't wait to see them," Leia said.

"Gotta go, Leia. Can I stop by Saturday at lunchtime?" he asked.

"That would be good. See you then," she said and smiled. She waved him off.

Leia finished up with the horses. When she felt the duties were caught up, and finished, she glanced over at the corral of cattle. She still didn't know how many heads there were. Brandon would probably tell her.

She left and returned to her newly painted little house. She made her mother dinner. Her mom had made her a fruit pie with fresh fruit from aunt Lilly. It smelled so good. She couldn't wait to have a piece with some vanilla ice cream she had bought last week.

Her mom did okay while she was gone for three hours but that is about the longest she could ever leave her. That night Billie needed extra pain pills so Leia gave them to her.

That night after a good hot shower and a supper around a campfire Carlos and Tracy had made, Brandon put his body to bed. He wanted to dream about Leia, as he'd just seen her that day, but no thoughts breezed in his mind as he fell fast asleep in the bunkhouse.

Chapter Six

The boss came to the barn early Monday morning and explained the plan for the week. The vet was there too. The cattle were to be caught up on any shots and protection warranted against diseases. This would take two days and then they would herd them through the ranch to another elevation, which would take two days maybe three. Everyone was needed for this excursion, Carlos said. "You'll be camped out at night, so bring blankets, etc. and camp equipment with you. I'll have the horse pack for food and other supplies."

One of the gals spoke up asking, "This is like a pack trip in the movies, right? Just like in the old westerns, huh?"

"I'm afraid it is. There is coyote, and other wild animals we might encounter. We don't shoot. Just scare 'em off. I'll bring some flares, and, of course, we'll have the camp fire and horses," Carlos said like he'd done this a thousand times. Except he hadn't.

The three lead hands would organize everyone else. Carlos didn't see a problem. He told them, "Just keep the pack tight, and try not to bust any standing fences. Wednesday morning they'd set out and return Friday before sundown. They would cross one road as his property was on the other side of the highway.

Brandon prepared for the pack trip condensing as much as possible. Actually they didn't need much, just some warmer clothes to add on at night with a few edibles and drinks.

In the morning, he put his boots on which were getting their share of usage lately, and he added a vest over his shirt, one of the experienced hands had given him. He looked in the mirror. Yep, he looked like a cowboy. Leia should see him. He should send his sister and her family a picture. He'd get one of the guys to take a pic and he'd send it to her email in a few days.

He was saving every cent he made for two things, well, maybe three. He wanted to buy a cell phone, property for a farm and the third thing … he wanted to take Leia on a date. He was going to do that this Saturday.

Once he got to the barn after a quick egg-sandwich breakfast and coffee, he put the equipment on his horse including the blanket, saddle, the strap and adjusted the stirrups. They used a different stirrup today, called the oxbow, as it was preferred with cattle.

He loaded up his pack of extras and tied up, Thunder, outside near the horse corral.

Everyone was getting ready and Carlos said they'd leave shortly. Carlos had a big smile on his face. This was his land and his herd, and oh, his hands. He looked like a proud ranch owner. His kids were out running around this morning, insisting they were qualified to ride with him.

Aspen, the oldest had dark hair almost waist length. Autumn and Montana were twins, who had their hair in braids the color of golden hay. The last little one, named Tallulah, wore her hair pixie style and she was the spitting image of Carlos, who was as handsome as they come with dark brown eyes and a dimpled chin. They were pulling and yelling at their dad, begging to let them come along. One of them even said, "We are going to miss you and momma cannot get along without you."

Momma came out to retrieve her brood and corral them in from all the pleading. She repeated, "When you are older, I will let you go, after you show me your horse riding skills and camping skills, too."

The two guides at the front were the more experienced hands with one of them coming around giving encouragement and orders to the rest of the hands. The pack trip was on and moving. Brandon was at the tail, he wasn't sure if this was good or not. He rode with Carlos and one of the gals. He finally learned how many head of cattle Carlos had purchased.

Carlos had purchased 600 head with 200 of them belonging to Tracey's brother. They would all range together, though. For two days and nights the ranch hands did nothing but eat, sleep and drive cattle. At the end, they felt experienced and invigorated. All was good.

On Friday night he crawled into bed and felt like he'd laid on a king's bed.

When Saturday came Brandon went to town and walked into the flower shop. He wanted to give Leia a few flowers. He spotted the Indian paintbrush and had the lady wrap it with some greenery adorned with a red-green plaid ribbon.

"Someone special getting these?" asked the lady behind the counter.

He smiled politely.

"They are for a friend. I'm going there for lunch," Brandon said and paid her.

He showed up and knocked on her back door. She let him in. He joined her in the kitchen with her mother at the wooden table. Then he looked around and he was stunned. It looked like a brand new place, "Whoa, the place looks great. Show me the rest."

"Sweetie, show him the house. I'll work on lunch," said Billie.

Leia became excited for all she had done, especially, when Brandon exaggerated and seemed truly inspired by her paint job.

"It looks wonderful. I bet the place hadn't had paint in fifty years. Does it cheer you up knowing you did all this work?" he asked her.

"Oh my. It does. You cannot believe how it made me feel accomplished, though, not like Van Goh or anything. It made me own it, even though it's not mine," she said. "Does that make any sense at all?"

"I think I can comprehend. I don't own anything, either, but I do take care of my little area in the bunkhouse. I even sweep the floor and keep the tiny kitchen cleaned up," he said.

"Maybe it comes from all the hard work out here, from all the farming and feeding of the animals. Possibly, the wide open spaces between houses, and ranches, gets in your skin and becomes spiritual like."

"Things are pretty simple out here, aside from the hard labor and all the muscle building," he said and laughed.

She'd taken him on a tour throughout both levels of the house. It was a two story traditional, old farmhouse about ready to buckle. When they returned to the kitchen, mother had everything ready. She'd put the spaghetti and meatballs out and buttered some garlic bread. She even added a salad with homegrown carrots, onions and a green tomato. The only reason the first two ingredients were ready was she and Leia had started them inside in March from seeds.

"What would you like to drink?" Billie asked.

"What do you have?" He asked in return.

"I've got milk, sweet tea, cherry juice, water and coffee."

"Cherry juice sound good with ice if you have some," he replied.

"Sure thing, coming right up," said Billie.

"I can get it if you need me to," he said quickly.

"No, please, I do quite a bit in this chair on wheels. I just don't walk anymore," she said.

"You do seem to get around pretty well. How's the pain?" Leia had told him she had quite a bit; sometimes it got real bad that she almost screamed.

"A couple time a week it gets unbearable and Leia puts me to bed with a couple pain pills," she issued quietly. They ate the simple Italian style dinner in the tiny kitchen.

"My bones are getting weak from no walking or exercise, only my arms have strength now," she spoke the truth.

Leia was quiet as she had nothing to say.

"I'm boring you two. You are finished, go outside and get some air. I'll clean up," Billie remarked.

She watched them walk out in the grass towards the backfields, beyond the cottonwood tree where her life ended. She was truly sad over her dear husband's passing. Why did he do that? They should have left Wyoming and headed south, found easier jobs than what they'd done for forty years or more.

A handful of bad years and bad loans sunk them. There was nothing anyone could do. It was a shame, everyone said so, but no one could help. This world mostly looked out for the all mighty dollar. She shouldn't feel bitter, but one could hardly feel any different especially when it took someone you loved.

Her husband's heart was tied to this ranch; he loved it dearly and so did Leia. She supposed that's why Leia was still here, for the ranch and to take care of her. Poor girl had to look out after her mother and for how long? Billie felt the burden she was for her daughter as she looked out the window. This was the first guy Leia had ever even looked at. She was twenty-three and so beautiful. She deserved a life. She vowed she would let her have it, even if her own was nonexistent.

He almost forgot and told her to wait right there. He ran to the truck and retrieved his flowers. He came back and said, "These are for you, the Indian paintbrush, but they came from the flower shop in town."

"How sweet of you to remember, the color of the plains and our state flower," she said and smiled.

"I've planned our date next Saturday. I hope you don't mind," Brandon stated.

"Not at all. Are you going to tell me? Or will it be a surprise?" she asked.

"Do you like surprises?"

She looked at him and seemed puzzled. Then she said, "Yes, I want to be surprised!"

He took her hand and they walked on the plains for a small eternity. Mesmerized and happy with one another, the pair was oblivious to the vastness of space.

Leia could hardly wait for Saturday, *it needed to be here already,* she thought. As she waited she assisted her mother who seemed rather down this week. She tried to cheer her but couldn't. She asked for extra pain pills, and Leia told her the bottle was getting low. She needed a replacement so as not to run out of them.

Leia worked on making a dress for herself for Saturday. Aunt Lilly had given her some very smart material, and she wanted to look good. She knew she would wear boots and maybe even a cowboy hat. She had one that Carlos had given her last Christmas. She just hadn't had a place to wear it yet. It was a Stetson and a soft grey color with braiding and a blue feather. It was mighty fine; yes, it was smart!

Brandon was up before anyone else on Saturday morning in the bunkhouse. He had a date, as in all day date. She didn't know where he was taking her. Later, they would be going to a park he'd looked into. It had a river and walking trails. The park guide said it was scenic.

He had Marissa, the lady bartender from the Painted Pony make him a picnic basket for two. She did this for customers, and he had heard they were worth the money. Brandon also bought a bottle of white wine, and had chilled it in a cooler in the back of the truck. He had put everything together for a first date. His anticipation made him smile. Certainly she would be as enthralled as him.

"Hurry up, Leia, or you won't be ready!" Her mother yelled up at her. Billie could see the truck coming up towards the house. The dust was flying behind him. It was Brandon and he was on time. She smiled to herself thinking about days of long ago. She must remember to ask Leia for a couple pills and water before she left. Her sister would be a little late today, but that was okay, she told Leia. She could be here by herself for a short time.

A knock was heard at the door and Billie hollered, "Come on in. She's about ready."

"Good morning, Mrs. Settles," Brandon greeted Leia's mother.

"Yes. Morning to you to," Billie retorted.

In walked Leia and both of them didn't quite know what to say, but they both smiled and Billie nodded her approval.

"Leia's been teaching herself to sew. Honey, you did real well. It looks store bought, even better," Billie said, complimenting her daughter.

"That is incredible! You taught yourself to sew. Did you learn from a book?" he asked.

"No, but I probably should have. My aunt Lilly gave me the material and I first practiced making some dolls' clothes. I did buy a couple patterns, but also I found you can take apart other clothes," she said.

"What do you mean take apart other clothes?" He asked. He truly wondered about this idea.

"I disconnected the stitching from some items that I got at Goodwill. Then, I replicated 'em," Leia said rather proudly.

"You're a genius," he said.

"Are you teasing me?" she pondered.

"No. You did that?" Brandon seemed curious at how she made her new dress.

"Do you like it?" She twirled about in the kitchen for both of them to see.

"Yeah, I really like it," he said.

The dress did turn out, despite the initial troubles she had with the machine. The red floral design was set against a black background. She supposed it reminded her of the Indian paintbrush flower. She had used the peasant type blouse she owned and combined it with a skirt. The two put together gave her a floral dress with a peasant top and mini dress. She wore boots and brought along her lady Stetson.

She had never been this dressed up before, except when she went to her dad's funeral. They'd gone out to dinner in Cheyenne, somewhere fancy and everyone ordered steak. Somebody else paid for i, because she and her mom were broke. Money was tight, especially since Leia was the main caregiver, and couldn't have a full time job. The ranch was supposed to be their full time employment, their forever career. Somehow, that didn't work out.

Brandon and Leia got ready to go and Billie told them to wait a minute. She went to the kitchen cupboards and pulled out a container. "I know you are going on a date and Brandon is supposed to pay for everything, but I want to give both of you something.

Brandon, take this and just have a little extra fun at whatever you are going to do. I'd like to think Leia's dad would approve and want you to have a good time, too," she said. She'd given him fifty bucks. It was her private stash she kept in the kitchen, the emergency money.

He tried to give it back, but realized quickly Billie wanted to do this. He'd learned from his uncle, adults do this. They mean it. Don't give it back. If they wanted it they wouldn't do it in the first place.

Leia climbed into his truck and he shut the door behind her, and then climbed in himself. He turned the truck on and adjusted the radio. He looked over at her and asked her if she knew where they were going.

"I have an idea but I won't say," she said and laughed.

"Fair enough," he responded and pulled away.

The music played and with the windows rolled down life suddenly seemed easy. The wind blew her hair into her eyes. She didn't care.

It was easy to be with Brandon, he was carefree and easy to talk with. He had good manners and a pretty smile. Her mom liked him. She could tell. She knew he was a hard worker as the ranch hands had given Carlos a good report. He was well liked.

But she didn't want to think about any of that, she wanted to find out what it was like to be with Brandon. What was it like to hang out with him the whole day?

She was about to find out.

Chapter Seven

Brandon and Leia spent the day at the rodeo. She had guessed right. They watched the barrel races, the clown show and several others. The pair took in the singing show and checked out the animals. The place was more like a fair than just a rodeo. Rides and games and lots of eats n treats were everywhere.

It was about two o'clock and Brandon said, "Leia, I have another surprise."

"You do?" she asked.

"Unless you want to stay at the rodeo, I thought we would go check out one of the state parks," he said, hoping she would say yes.

"A state park? Do you have a picnic planned or are we walking some dusty trails?" she inquired.

"There's a park that has all of that. I thought we could see the river and walk some on the trails," he replied and laughed.

"I'd love to do that," she said.

"Great, let's go," Brandon said. He took her hand and hurriedly left for the truck.

She felt the connection as their hands touched and he squeezed her tightly. He felt like running, but didn't. He was happy and he couldn't erase the smile that seemed to be growing with each step. He looked over at her and Leia was smiling, too. She gave him a flirty look with her eyes, at least it looked that way to him.

Once they arrived at the park and drove through the long entrance, they came upon a large lake and nearby river. Picnic tables and a day campsite were also there. He climbed out of the truck and she followed. He lifted a canvas cover off of his picnic supplies.

"I'm going to carry the large backpack with the supplies. Can you carry this smaller pack?" Brandon asked her.

"Sure, how far are we going?" Leia asked.

"Just a couple miles," he said and continued, "You okay with that?"

"Yes, but only because I wore the right boots," she said. She had worn her old boots that felt like slippers on her feet.

"Let's get started as we'll have to come back before dark, you know when all the wild animals come out," he said and raised his eyebrows.

"Are you trying to scare me?" She'd lived out here all her life and wasn't going to suddenly get scared. Though the thought of being out in the wilderness at night didn't exactly thrill her either.

"Never, I just wanted you to know our plans and the park closes at dark," he said.

It was a beautiful day in June and Wyoming was breathtaking, especially when you got away from the roads and people. It was pure land filled with rocks and brush and the river singing its song as it gushed past you. They strode one in front of the other walking the trail next to the river. The river was blue and clear with white caps where it gleaned over the rocks underneath.

Someday she would like to take a raft trip. She always wanted to do that. She'd heard the rivers in Colorado were perfect, but Wyoming had some rapids especially after a big winter. She thought to herself maybe she could plan that; maybe Brandon would like that. He seems like the adventurous type.

He found a spot and pointed to it. There was a bend in the river where it turned its course to the right and continued on. He put the pack down and unloaded the supplies he'd brought. He set up a campfire as small fires were allowed in these designated areas. She pulled the blanket out and he handed her the picnic basket that he purchased with goods inside from the Painted Pony in town.

The couple talked for a while and then laid back and looked at the sky before sharing the food and drink. They actually fell asleep and Brandon woke up first and startled Leia, "I think we better eat this picnic before any more time goes by. I'm hungry anyway, are you?"

"Yeah, what did she pack for you?" she asked.

"Two bison burgers with the works on the side!" he assured her.

A day by the river was sublime thought Brandon. He should do this more often. The both of them were calm and not worried. They'd also shared a bottle of wine that Brandon bought. They talked about their families and their lives when they were children growing up, remembering little nuances of childhood. In essence, they got to know each other just a little more.

The drive home in the truck was befitting to the peaceful day they had shared. A glorious sunset was in the making. As he drove the large rose colored ball before them was making its way down the skyline into the horizon. Brandon put his shades on.

He pulled in and drove the gravel road to take her home. He stopped but left the keys in the ignition. He left the radio playing, too. She looked at him and he turned in her direction. They both knew what was coming. He kissed her for a thousand seconds. He could feel his own heartbeat as it pumped against his chest. She touched his face and didn't let go. He graced her hand and held it in his as he left go of their first kiss. Nothing was finer that evening at dusk in the truck outside Leia's broken house.

A week later, on the 4th of July, Leia had no plans. She was going to watch TV with her mother, a digital fireworks display in her family room. After dark she heard a knock on the back door and she could see Brandon standing there.

"They let you out from the ranch?" she asked.

"Barely any time off, but I wanted to share a few fire works with you.

I bought some sparklers and a couple other items from the store," he said.

"Sure, let me grab something for us to drink," she said and took two beers from the fridge.

They sat on the back cement stoop, after she'd turned off the kitchen lights, and lit up the sparklers. She held both of the sparklers. When he returned from lighting one of the cans with a few rocket style colors that would spew in the air, she could see the sparkler's reflection in his eyes. She was mesmerized.

"Happy 4th of July," he said. She returned the saying.

"I really came back for another kiss," he said and turned to see the most beautiful girl he'd ever met waiting for their second kiss.

Chapter Eight

July and August came and went as they were laden with long, dusty hot days filled with chores from the barn to the fields. Crops and cattle called relentlessly. Then Tracey purchased a small buffalo herd in mid-August. The meat was in demand and he thought he should try that, too. He wanted to make this ranch work, to be ahead of the game, and not lose it like his predecessor had.

September and October had plenty of chores to a lesser degree. The days were still busy just not hot and not as long. The bunkhouse had lost a few hands so the ones left were busy enough.

Brandon was able to save his money and he had a nice stash now. He barely did anything and ate up at the house any chance he could in addition to the five meals a week. He liked their family, and they had invited him up to the house for the holidays in November and December. He decided to take them up on it and maybe go visit his sister in January or February. He'd been gone a year.

Once December came chores were half a day at most, so they had extra time. He went to visit Leia and hung out with her.

Billie had decided she wouldn't bother with the Christmas decorations this year and Leia asked her why. "Mom, why don't you want me to get the box out? We do it every year."

"Leia, I don't know. You and Brandon maybe ought to spend time together at the main ranch house with all the kids and decorations up there," she said.

Leia sensed her mom just didn't want to bother. "Mom, yeah we could do that, but I still live here so I want to have a little tree. You know with lights and ornaments to get us in the Christmas spirit."

"The Christmas spirit, yes, I suppose we should be in the spirit," she said but looked away out the back window towards the large cottonwood tree.

When Brandon came over that day, she asked him if he would take her out to get a small tree and help her decorate it. They spent the day doing just that.

"Tomorrow when your aunt Lilly comes can you come over to the main house? I've been invited to help them decorate the big tree with the kids and bake some cookies. It should be fun," he asked Leia.

"Aw, I would love to," she responded like sugar melting into a favorite cup of coffee.

"Good, we're invited for dinner, too."

Before leaving the house Saturday morning after her aunt Lilly arrived, Leia spoke with her mother. She told her she'd been invited to dinner and asked if she minded. She asked how long aunt Lilly was staying.

"Leia, Lilly is going to stay with me until tomorrow, so you don't have to rush home tonight. I won't need you here so please enjoy the kids and the dinner. They'll probably even have a bonfire outside and roast some marshmallows. Kids love that," Billie said like a mother who knew all about children.

Leia dressed warm with boots that had fur tucked inside and put on her warmest coat, just in case they would be outside by the bonfire. When Brandon came he brought her mother a wreath for the door, it was made of fresh greens and had leaves and other woodsy items adorned with a big ribbon that was tied in a bow.

"This is for you and Leia," he handed the wreath to her mom and smiled.

"Thank you Brandon, how kind of you," Billie said. Her eyes glossed over just a bit.

"The kids up at the main house made it. The tree, season, state and river gorge (names of the kids) all put their hands and hearts upon it," he chuckled.

"Brandon," Leia said and shook her head.

Aspen, Autumn, Montana, and Tallulah greeted Leia and Brandon and the others from the bunkhouse, welcoming them into their home like family. They wanted their attention and they would have it. As soon as they were in the door, the tree decorating began, and other crafts got started in the kitchen. Keri had this all under control.

In the kitchen the little elves got busy with making bows for more wreaths. Keri had a small seasonal business of making wreaths and home goods, which she would sell up in town at one of the local shops.

Leia got started with the cookie and baked goods section in the kitchen, and Brandon helped the kids with the ladder and hanging the highest ornaments on the top of the tree. Tracey had adapted many traditional routines when it came to Christmas as she had been exposed to more than her Native American ways. She tried to make sure Christmas wasn't all about presents, but inclusion of both ideas and certainly about family and joy.

When she was growing up someone had showed her how to make garland for the Christmas tree. She learned how to string popcorn and make a cranberry string.

Right before dinner and after the tree was decorated, they all came in the kitchen and gathered around the table. Several strings were laid out, and each grabbed an end. The older kids began to string the cranberries.

Autumn turned some seasonal music on which filled the large house with sounds of the season. Small flakes were falling outside, nothing settling on the ground. Soon though, thought Tracy, it would snow hard and lots of it.

After the kids got tired of stringing the cranberries, the adults took over and sat around finishing up. They set them aside to put on the tree after dinner before the marshmallow roast.

Tracy had been cooking the meat slow all day and they had barbeque pork sandwiches and creamed corn with cookies for dessert. It was a couple weeks until Christmas, but all the decorating and baking was complete.

After dinner and out by the fire, Tracey pulled out his guitar and sang a few songs that everyone might know. He also played a couple that no one had ever heard before.

The children went into the house and off to bed, then the couple walked arm in arm and strolled around watching it snow, tasting a few flakes along the way.

They walked into the barn to check on the horses and get warmer. "You know my aunt Lilly is staying with my mom tonight, so you don't have to take me back, if you don't want to," she said.

He looked at her and then looked around, wondering where they could possibly sleep and stay warm. "You think you might like to sleep in the barn with the animals?"

"Well, we could. We did that as kids, plenty of times," she said, remembering.

"Always an adventure out here in Wyoming, isn't it?" he asked. "Let me go to the bunkhouse to get some blankets, as I'm pretty sure the temperature is going down."

As the children lay sleeping in their warm beds up in the main house, Brandon and Leia slept in the barn that night with blankets and coats all around them. Leia declared to herself that she was in love and she would tell him.

After they walked around, trying to find the warmest spot in the barn, they made their place to sleep. She shivered just a little, not because she was cold, but because she was nervous.

"You okay?" he asked.

"I am. Are you?" she asked in return.

"I need to tell you something before time goes on," he started. "I came out here to learn something. To find something, something maybe I didn't know how to do."

"And have you found maybe what you wanted to learn?" she asked.

"Yes, but I found something, something even more. I found someone I wasn't expecting to meet." He paused to find the right words.

She swallowed as she hoped to hear something she felt herself.

"Leia, I found you and I can't stop thinking about you. I want to be with you," he said as softly as he could speak without whispering.

"I think about you all the time, since the first day I met you in town by the store," she uttered breathlessly.

He smiled, garnered his courage and looked at her again with intensity, "I love you, Leia. I know I do. And this makes me happy," he said and felt relief. This burden of love he carried in his heart had been spoken. It was the truth.

"I love you, too, Brandon Smith. I really do."

Chapter Nine

Christmas had been fantastic for Tracey and Keri at the Settles Ranch. The kids behaved and they had a myriad of celebrations. Their parents had come for a couple days and hours of endless game playing, and reviewing of the ranch activities kept everyone busy. Most of the hands had gone home to families except for Brandon and two others from Mexico. Jesus and Ralph stayed on and celebrated with Brandon, and, of course, Leia.

On Christmas Day, Leia and Brandon, went for a snowmobile ride over the countryside and enjoyed the view, a 360-degree panorama, which went on for miles. Once they went up in elevation, the climatic emotion of awe was stunning, breathtaking. She held on and felt comforted as she let him be in control, and take them across the barren white farmland.

They had exchanged gifts but nothing of any seriousness for it had only been six or seven months since they'd met. Things were just getting going and a destination or a plan towards that was not revealed. They were still in the exploration phase of dating.

Leia told Brandon she'd be busy with her mom for a couple weeks as her Aunt was leaving town on a vacation. He said he'd try to stop by and visit; maybe he could help her with her mother and give her a break. She liked that idea and welcomed him to do just that.

Brandon came over December 31st and spent the entire day and evening. He gave Leia the keys to the truck so she could go in town and do the shopping. She made a list for a special dinner, and even bought champagne to toast at midnight. Brandon had given her some extra money. He stayed back, and took care of her mom. He put her to bed for a nap, lifting her out of the wheelchair as her arms had become weak, and she needed this extra assistance.

He gave her the two pain pills she took at mid-day with a fresh glass of water. Once he did these things, he saw how, Billie, was so dependent upon, Leia, every day.

"When should I come back? I mean how long will you be napping?" he asked Billie.

"Brandon, come back in about two hours, maybe three. I'll be here, dear. I'm not going anywhere," Billie responded.

"Okay, Mrs. Settles. Will do."

"It's Billie, call me Billie. You've seen enough of me to call me by my first name," she remarked rather kindly.

"Billie, see you in a couple hours. I'll be right out here, just holler," he said and he felt pity for Leia's mom. This arthritis and bone crippling was bad news, for sure.

While Billie slept on New Year's Eve Day, the two of them made one recipe after another. You'd think they were getting ready for a party of ten or more. The mess made in the kitchen seemed like a party itself as the couple enjoyed this time to themselves.

"It's New Year's. Do you make resolutions?" he asked Leia.

"No, not really. For me it's just another evening here," she revealed sadly.

"I'm sorry," he said.

"Please, don't be. I don't really know any different. I love my mom and she needs me badly. She's very sweet and loves me. She actually misses dad so much. I think it kills her slowly, every day."

"She does need you, a lot," he replied.

She hadn't meant to reveal so much but he was so kind. He understood her dilemma.

Someday, she would go and get a real job when mom didn't need her she thought.

"How's those dresses you were making this summer? Did you make any more to sell?" he inquired.

"I did make about ten this fall. Keri is going to sell them this spring in town. The donation store in town may even let me sell them there. If I donate some, the charity may pay me a small amount to sell them at a discount. They said that would benefit both of us, and help me to get started making and selling dresses," she explained.

"Good for you. Sounds like a plan," he said with glee.

"Do you make resolutions?" she asked him.

"I have made them before and mostly nothing happens, so this time I'm making none," Brandon said.

She looked at him and didn't know what to say. She became speechless. She turned away and looked for something to do. She didn't know how she felt. He always seemed so motivated and driven, he'd always had a plan of some sort.

The rest of the day and night could not have gone any better, thought Brandon.

They toasted at midnight in the kitchen. They stopped playing cards and watched the television as it dropped some object down at the count of ten. Even Billie stayed up for the occasion. She then insisted he sleep on the couch and leave in the morning. There was no sense in driving tonight with the snow and all. He might get stuck or something.

Leia put her mom to bed and kissed her, said goodnight and 'happy new year' again. She told her to sleep in just a bit, maybe an extra hour since they had stayed up so late.

"Thanks honey, I will. Good night to you and Happy New Year, to you and Brandon." Billie laid her head on the pillow and soon fell asleep.

In the morning, Brandon, left Leia a note. She knew he had to leave early and drive Ralph and Jesus in town to meet some folks. He kissed her cheek and left a note on the kitchen table.

He thanked them for a wonderful day and night. He ended it with

'The New Year has begun, so be it. Now let's get busy living. Bye, Brandon."

Little did he know as he walked out that door, it would be the last time.

Chapter Ten

Brandon sat at the Painted Pony and ordered lunch. He'd dropped his fellow bunkhouse mates off at the bowling alley as they were meeting up with some folks from their homeland. The music from his Uncle Sam's shop played on the jukebox. He thought about him and his sister and all her kids. He imagined him and Leia dancing to these serene and classic tunes. He smiled.

Marissa waited on him and served him a sandwich with sauerkraut in it. He remembered from Sam that kraut was good luck on New Year's Day. It was one of those traditions that you did, but didn't necessarily believe.

He still hadn't bought a phone; he needed to do that. Brandon borrowed Marissa's phone and called his sister back in Chicago. He had spoken to her on Christmas Day and talked with each of his nieces and nephew. Her husband Josh sounded overwhelmed with five kids but at least he had a job. He worked for the city doing construction of roadways and bridges and their subsequent repair.

Brandon looked outside and it had started to snow again. He noticed the wind had picked up considerably. *Probably a storm was coming,* he thought. He looked up at the television as Marissa had changed the station to the news. Forecasts of a winter blizzard were in full broadcast.

He dialed his sister. As soon as Sam, his uncle, answered the phone he knew something wasn't right. He froze a bit before he asked, "Sam, is it you?"

"Brandon, thank God. I'm so glad you called."

A long pause worried Brandon immediately.

"Why are you answering Riley's phone?" he asked.

"Brandon, I'm here with the kids. Her neighbor is here, too," he replied. He took a deep breath and continued. "There has been an accident, a tragedy actually. Please sit down."

"I'm sitting, Sam. I'm sitting. What? Tell me, please," Brandon said and looked around. He looked outside at the swirling white flakes.

"Brandon, Josh was killed last night."

"What? Oh no!" he said. He knew there was more. He waited for Sam.

"Your sister is alive, but there's more. I've been trying to reach you, but no one has a number out there, only the letters you've sent."

"Can I talk with her? Put her on the phone, she must be beside herself. Are the kids okay?" he asked, rambling on and on. Wondering how she was coping.

"She's not here. I need you to come home. Can you do that?" Sam asked.

Brandon sat still with no words. He held the phone but was silent. Inside he knew what he would do, but his heartbeat told him his loss didn't matter at this single moment in time.

"I can. When?" he whispered.

"Brandon, you are the only family she has. You know that and they have no money, no insurance and five kids. Welfare will help a little, but these kids need someone or they'll split them up," he said, trying to give him a picture of the future, to see the importance.

"She needs me for a while. Certainly, I'll come. I think there is a storm brewing, a snowstorm," Brandon looked at the television again.

"Son. I'm sorry, but it's far worse," Sam said. Brandon could hear him sob into the phone.

Brandon braced himself and swallowed hard. He'd just had a great

Christmas and today was New Year's Day. And now, he was receiving this terrible news to which he must respond.

"She's hurt badly. She's in the intensive care unit with a breathing tube and hasn't woke up yet," Sam managed to say.

Brandon cried.

"Brandon, take the train back. Come home. Please, right away," he said, solemnly.

Brandon gave the phone back to Marissa and went over to a table. Quickly, he figured out what to do. What he had to do. He went to the general store and purchased a card for Leia. Then he went to the bank. He walked quickly back to the bar, drank another beer, and left for the train station, after giving the keys to Jesus. He'd have to send his boss a letter.

Jesus returned the truck and told his boss that Brandon had to go back home, as they needed him to help with the family. Tracey didn't like it because Brandon was one of his best hands. He liked the young man. He thought he would stay on longer than that. But he knew people came and went in this business. They were always looking for something else. He was glad to have him for as long as he had. Maybe he'd come back by June.

News of Brandon reached Leia. She wondered why he took off like that and didn't tell her. She missed him and hoped they would have continued seeing one another. In secret, she was devastated, but had hopes he might still come back, maybe even in the summer.

Winter continued with its blustery, cold winds that chapped the face and chilled the bones.

Tracey finally received notice from Brandon. He thanked him for his time out on the ranch and his generosity. He told him to say hello to Leia. He would not be returning to the ranch and his time was now taken. Tracey passed this on to Leia.

Leia received the hello and the other news that he would not return to the ranch. This made her sad but she couldn't think about it too long, as every day she was busy tending to her mother.

The snow lay on the ground all winter, and it piled up very high. She'd lost her phone line, so any calls from Brandon went unheard. Winter became dismal, and the only break was from her aunt Lilly.

If she could only get a job, she thought. She needed to have someone look after her mother, so she could get out and make some money. She continued to make dresses from the material her Aunt provided. Hope. She had hope she might sell them in the spring.

The money from her mother's check didn't stretch, but it did give them food and utilities.

She wrote Brandon a letter but didn't have an address. She would have to find out if the ranch had his address.

She saw on television where the Painted Pony was sold after the owner died from a heart attack, and it wouldn't reopen until summer or later. Winters were hard on the locals. Very little money flowed into the town.

By the end of February she knew. She found herself in a predicament for which she didn't have an answer. Leia put her hand to her stomach and took a deep breath. She looked out the window while a shiver ran up her spine at her own life. What would she do with another life? She needed a little time to figure this one out. For the mean time she would tell no one.

She bought a kit at a store on the other side of town, one she didn't frequent. At home she performed the steps, *pretty easy* she thought. Sure enough it was positive. She threw it in the garbage. She remembered from school one of her friends' sisters had gotten pregnant and didn't show for like six months. Maybe, she could hide it for a while, especially from her mother.

During the long white winter Keri would send someone over in the truck to pick her up to go to the store for groceries, whereas in the summer she would walk twice a week to town, and walk back home. Sometimes she'd catch a ride. The time alone was good for her; she escaped the doldrums of living in the old weathered house with her mother. Tracy also came by on Sundays with a huge amount of food from their Sunday dinner. Keri was a good cook, and always made way too much. She was thankful for that.

Chapter Eleven

eia didn't know it but her mother was becoming increasingly despondent. She'd been saving up her pain pills anyway, and hiding them in a secret area of her bedside drawer, unbeknownst to Leia. Why was she doing this? She wasn't really sure. She thought she was saving them for a rainy day, a just in case moment. After all why did her husband go out back and kill himself? Well, she knew the answer to that. He was depressed. He'd lost it all, every single acre he worked so hard on all his life, and he was left with nothing. Who could blame him? No one did.

But Billie, she was a nice soul. What she really worried about was her little girl. She shouldn't have to stay here, and take care of her in a wheelchair. Where was this boyfriend of hers? Why did he leave? He should have known better than to do this to Leia. These were the thoughts that overcame her mind endlessly, every day.

One day last summer when she saw Leia and Brandon sitting on the back stoop together, she had a thought as she looked out the window upon the large cottonwood. The death tree. She guessed it just hit her. She didn't plan it and never would have thought it in a million years. But her wheelchair, her little girl and the picture of her dead husband under the cottonwood tree, *just made for a perfect storm*, she thought.

Just like him, she didn't think about Lilly or Leia and the hurt they might suffer or how God would judge her. She thought only of the path that would lighten the others load.

And so her path was noted and she felt relieved with her plan. She'd saved all the pills for a few months, suffering the pain in silence. She would visit the cottonwood tree come this July, well before her daughter would have a baby. She'd found the pregnancy stick and saw it positive. She was waiting for Leia to tell her. She wondered when that might be. She would. She was just giving it some time to sink in. She knew her daughter.

The young man, Brandon, had left. Left her and gone back to where he came from. He'd left in a hurry on New Year's Day. She thought herself a good judge of character and he seemed like a good young man. He'd sent Leia a letter, but Billie kept it from her, she needed to let her plan take effect, and then they could be together. Leia would never leave Billie and Billie knew this.

Billie smiled to herself. This was for everyone's good.

"Mom, I brought you another blanket, it's getting down below zero outside and here is your pain pills," Leia said, and waited.

"Okay, thanks," Billie responded. "You can go now."

"No, go ahead and take them, and I'll take the glass as I'm doing a little cleanup," she said, and waited.

That was a first, waiting for her mom to take them. She'd surprised Billie with that, but she had no idea. Well, she wouldn't be in any pain this afternoon, she'd probably sleep right through it.

About an hour later, Billie opened her eyes and saw him. Her husband's ghost floated in the room, the window was open, and the curtains were swaying. Billie shivered. She shook her head a little to and fro, and batted her eyelashes. Swirling around the ceiling, and going from side to side of her bed was a slithery stream of white silky consciousness. She wasn't even scared, until she heard her name being called out. Then she screamed aloud.

In came Leia, running, and then quickly going to the window to close it. She looked at her mother, and she looked as though she'd seen a ghost or a monster. She was pale and diaphoretic, and when she clasped her hands they were clammy.

"Mother!" she exclaimed.

213

Chapter Twelve

*L*eia woke, and sat up in bed just as the wave of nausea overtook her slight features. She ran to the bathroom, careful not to make much noise, as she still kept this condition from her mother. No sense in worrying her. She'd probably have a stroke or something.

One day she just couldn't take it anymore, and she called the ranch to see if someone could pick her up, and bring her over to see Keri.

Once she was there, she took comfort in the kindness of this woman who seemed to have it all together. She was so organized. Everything was tidy and her kids were happy, running around playing games.

They sat in the kitchen and she made them both a cup of tea with ginseng and lemon. It warmed her insides and made her skin feel like it was glowing. Words came and the two caught up on all they had missed since Christmas.

"I want to work somewhere but something has come up and I need to tell someone something," she said and looked her straight in the eye. Keri looked and waited. "Keri, I'm going to have a baby. I need to make a plan. I'm not sure I can take care of mom and a baby. Do you think I can?" she asked this woman who was so capable.

"Leia, dear, you are. That's wonderful. When?" she asked her friend.

"I know. It is wonderful. Isn't it?" she replied.

"I've had four. I should know. I can give you all sorts of clothes, don't worry about clothes or cribs or anything like that," she said and rattled off a list of items.

"Thank you so much. I'm overwhelmed. I don't know what to say," she said.

"Have you been to the doctor?" she asked her.

"No. Not yet," she said.

"How far along are you?" she asked.

"I'm not sure but we were together before Christmas," she answered.

"It's Brandon's, the ranch hand who left to go home?" she quizzed.

"Yes," she simply said.

Keri smiled, and asked, "Does he know?"

"No, I haven't had a chance to let him know, but he went home and last I heard he is very busy. I want to get on my own two feet and not pressure him with this. I can't leave my mother all by herself, and move away. He may not even want me. I think I need some time to let this rest, and get used to this idea of being a mom," she spoke the truth from her heart.

"Of course, it is a big deal. A forever big deal."

"I have to tell my mother, very soon."

"Honey, she'll be okay with this. She's a good woman, a hard worker, and she loves you so much."

"I'm going to tell her when it warms up, in May. That's when I'll tell her. We can sit outside, and plan what we'll do," Leia said. She smiled, and began to dream just a bit, to envision what it might be like to have a baby.

"That sounds like a plan, but let me make a doctor's appointment for you because they like to see you early, and give you vitamins and such, to make sure the baby gets a real good start," Keri said, encouraging her friend.

"Okay, let me know when. Remember to keep it quiet for a little while," Leia said and smiled.

They both stood and Keri gave her friend a warm hug.

"Thanks for listening," Leia said and left. One of the ranch hands took her back, but not before Keri loaded her up with food, and made a call to her obstetrician. She wrote out the appointment on a card, and gave it to her.

A few days later Keri picked her up, and off they went. It was the end of March and she was three months pregnant. They did an assortment of lab tests and they got to see the heart beat on ultrasound. She was glad she went, and the female doctor assured her everything looked beautiful thus far. Expect a September 10th delivery, or thereabouts as that was her due date.

They left the office chatting and generally happy. "You should tell your mom, you know. She will be happy for you and she gets a grandchild," Keri spoke these words but wasn't so sure she believed them.

"It's okay, I'll let her know come May. The time is almost here and I want to keep this to myself, and not burden her yet.

The month of April Leia seemed to be rejuvenated. She had energy, and she was hungry. She sat at the table, and sewed one dress after another. Aunt Lilly brought her all kinds of fabric as some store in another city was going out of business. She brought her some patterns, too.

She experimented. It was actually fun. She was making something and just maybe she might make some money. She wasn't sure but the thought held her hopes high. Since she had to be here in the house, just maybe this plan might work out. Keri assured her the dresses would sell. She was negotiating with a charity in town to sell the dresses at a reduced fare, and Leia could keep the money from the sales. The charity would be helping her, and the women who needed a discounted clothing line. The ladies who managed this wanted to come out, and see her dresses.

"Could we come out the first Saturday in May to see them?" The lady asked Keri.

"I believe that would be just fine. Let me ask Leia."

"Just give me her address and we'll call her before we stop by," the woman said.

"She's two miles from the Settles Ranch. Her phone doesn't always work," she replied.

"That will do and I can't wait to meet her. Thank you Keri. Always a pleasure, hon."

May came and the very kind lady named Priscilla showed up, and knocked on Leia's door one Saturday. She was expecting her, and graciously allowed her come in. She had set about her dresses on hangars, and had them all over the three front rooms for her to view.

Leia offered her lemonade to drink and showed her the wares. The lady looked about going over each one and carefully checked the stitching and lengths. She took her time doing this and came back face to face with Leia, not even showing her a smile or whatever she thought.

Leia waited trying to read her face, wondering if it was worth all the hard work she had done. Billie came in via the wheelchair, and parked right next to her daughter. She waited alongside of her, and hoped she was giving a bit of support. Was she?

"These are nice. These are more than nice. Did you follow a pattern?"

"I altered the patterns, changed them around a little," Leia said.

"I know you did. I can see that," Priscilla said.

"So, do you want them for the charity store?" She asked. She decided to just come out with it.

Priscilla studied Leia for another moment, and then looked at her mother.

"I will sell these at the charity store starting next week. They will be discounted, as you know. I want you to come to the store one of these Saturdays and see what happens. We can talk then." Priscilla instructed her.

Leia nodded yes.

"Can you do that, sweetie?" she asked again.

"Oh, yes. I can do that."

Tears ran down Billie's cheeks which Leia didn't see.

219

Chapter Thirteen

eia made as many dresses as she could in several sizes, and sold them to Priscilla for the store in town. Priscilla wanted her to make more if she could before the end of June; she had another store in Wyoming and two in Colorado. She told her she thought they would sell. And so, Leia, worked on this, and went to the doctor with Keri to check on the baby.

She had told her mother about her pregnancy and her mother's reply was that she knew. Lillie told her that mother's just know these things. Billie asked her if she had told the father yet, or if she planned to.

"Mom, I am going too eventually. I don't want to put this upon him as we hadn't talked about the future, and then he left," Leia said. She wondered sometimes what he might say. She wanted to see the look on his face. After all, they were old enough. Both were in their early twenties and he was twenty-five, though, neither were self-reliant or independent.

"It is your business, but promise me you will tell him before next Christmas," said Billie.

"Why Christmas?" she asked.

"Babies are miracles, Leia. Some people can't ever have one and their hearts break. So remember, though you aren't married, they are still miracles bestowed upon big hearts. In other words, you will be giving much of yourself, for the baby for a long time. It takes time and money and love, lots of love, which I know you have. He deserves to know and the baby deserves to know where he came from, his or her roots, and genes. Promise me you'll let him know. He may even want to be a part of both of your lives," Billie lectured.

"Okay, mom. I will," Leia said.

Priscilla sent Leia cash in the mail, as she had requested, and Leia put it aside. She knew she had to save for the baby and whatever future she might have. She also had to come up with a plan and after much thinking; she knew she wouldn't go anywhere until after the birth. She would stay put and then maybe if her aunt Lilly would take her mother for a while, she'd take a trip. She didn't dwell on this idea very long, but it was proper to give him a chance and let him know.

Keri consistently mentioned to Leia about moving in with them, and helping to care for her family. Then she'd have a place to live. She thanked her for that and did consider it. She told her she would let her know.

July came and she received an envelope from Priscilla. It was a check this time with a little note. She read it and couldn't help but smiling. All her dresses were gone and the check was for $600. *There must be some mistake,* she thought. At the bottom of the note she read Priscilla's words. 'I'm sending an additional two hundred dollars in advance to make more dresses. Consider making ones with longer sleeves for the fall. Thanks, great job Leia!'

July 26th was an exceptionally beautiful day. The weather was sunny and 77 degrees. This morning she helped her mother with a bath and changed her bed linen. She even washed, and dried her hair, then curled it with a curling iron.

"You look good, mom."

"This old mop looks good?" she uttered.

"Yes. Here, look in the mirror," said Leia, lightly laughing.

It was a perfect morning. Leia made lunch, and they ate together at the kitchen table, laughing and talking, mostly about the baby. A few names came up and were quickly dismissed. Leia told her mom, she thought she might take a nap. She'd been through the spell of tiredness the first three months, and then the burst of continuous energy. Now though, she was five or six weeks away, and she grew more tired as her stomach expanded, too.

"Leia, you take a nap. I'd like to go sit outside, and read a book as the temperature seems perfect," she said, and wheeled herself towards the back. Leia helped her out the doorway and down the steps. Billie had her take her out to the large cottonwood beyond the small garage. Billie carried her drink with her and her book. They traversed over a few bumps along the way. The picture set as the obedient daughter wheeled her to the death tree, as Billie liked to call it.

Leia came in, and went upstairs to her room. She climbed under the covers, and fell fast asleep.

Meanwhile, Billie knew she shouldn't do what she was about to do, but she didn't see any other way. This would free Leia from this paramount responsibility she didn't deserve. Keri had invited her to live at the Settles Ranch. She would be taken care of, during and after the birth, and have a decent place to live with kind people.

The best part is she knew Brandon liked her. Once he knew, she'd bet her life on it, he'd come and be with her, or so she hoped. He had written her. And the final wish was that she made Leia promise she'd go, and tell him. Billie knew Leia would keep her promise. She smiled. She thought she had it all worked out.

She pulled out her container of pills, the pills she'd been saving since last year. She wasn't sure how many it would take, but she figured if twelve was the maximum for a day then fifty ought to do the deed. She hoped she had enough drink to finish off as many as she could. It took about ten minutes before she'd taken as many as possible and the drink was all gone. She hid the baggie in her pocket, and put the book across her lap. She closed her eyes, and drifted off, waiting for it to be all over.

Several hours passed, and Leia woke up groggy but quickly became aware. She looked at the time. She best check on her mother and think about dinner. She also had some laundry to do.

Leia decided to get the mail first. She called out to her mother telling her she'd be right there. She took the SUV out to the mailbox, which was by the road. She grabbed the mail and didn't read it, nothing important she figured and went back to her mother.

She noticed her mother's head was dipped forward like she was asleep. She decided it had been a long time, and she wouldn't sleep tonight if she let her go anymore.

Once Leia stood next to her, she noticed her hands had fallen to her side. "Mom. Time to wake up," Leia said.

She put her hands in her lap, and called out her name again. She was definitely not going to sleep tonight. She flipped the break off, turned her around, and headed toward the house. They hit a bump and Billie slid forward. When Leia stepped around to prevent her from falling out of the chair, the rest of her body fell from the chair to the ground. This didn't even wake her up.

"Mom, what's wrong? Wake up!" she yelled.

Still nothing. Leia dropped to the ground, and held her head touching her cheeks. She seemed lifeless. Something was wrong. She checked her breathing by looking at her chest. She didn't seem to be breathing.

God no. Leia began to feel her adrenaline kick in, and immediately checked her wrist for a pulse. Keri had taught her how to do this as she had taken a rescue course. She didn't feel anything, but she was unsure. Panic set in as in what to do.

She could give her a couple breaths, but she didn't know CPR, and the phone in the house had been cut off for three months. She'd have to take the four-wheeler or the topless jeep to the Settles Ranch. She'd have to leave her here. She couldn't do that.

She lay in the tall grass, holding her mother, and crying uncontrollably as tears streamed down her cheeks. Her mother's body was lifeless in her arms, while her own body carried life in its womb. This made no sense, "Mother, please don't leave me. Please come back."

An hour later she released her, and rose up. She went inside and got the keys to the jeep. She drove to the Settles Ranch, her previous home a long time ago, when things were happy and her parents were alive. Methodically, and with no emotion left, she did what she had to do.

Chapter Fourteen

*L*eia buried her mother the 29th of July, exactly three years after her father-committed suicide. She didn't know what the chances were of that happening. The cause of death was marked as probable heart attack, no one suspected overdose, even though it occurred on the same day. Leia suspected she missed him so much, her heart gave out, especially, sitting out there thinking about him on the anniversary of his death.

It was decided for Leia, immediately after the funeral, that she should live at the Settles Ranch. Tracey had told her he was changing the name, and the signage would be put up next month. Everything had gone through free and clear now. He owned the ranch through a cooperative of investors, but he was the man in charge. He really was beaming about this. He was excited and she was sad. She wanted to feel depressed but she was too busy being pregnant and helping Keri. There were so many chores.

The beginning of August came, and she prepared her room for her and the baby. She was told she could stay as long as she liked, there would be work for her here at the ranch. She knew horses, the barn, fieldwork, and she could learn more cooking and cleaning.

One day she ran into Marissa from the Painted Pony. Marissa told her she needed someone to cover a few lunches per week. The two of them discussed this, and Leia told her she would like to learn that in addition to the ranch. She was also still making dresses for Priscilla. Between the three she just might make an income to support the two of them. This pleased her.

She told her the baby's due date of September 10th and said she'd probably be ready about three weeks after. She thought so anyway.

On August 15th a baby boy she named Landon was born without any distress. He was healthy and came rather easily per the midwife. The whole delivery took two hours. Healthy cries from the little one and a robust suck on the bottle. Things seemed to be flowing free of worries for Leia and her new baby boy. She shared him with Tracey and Keri and the whole brood.

What a nice place to come home to from the hospital, a place filled with friendly smiles and warm embraces. She sighed and remembered her mother, who would miss out on all this, this miracle she brought into the world.

Aspen was extremely good at helping her with the baby. She was the oldest and seemed to know so much about babies, what they needed and when they needed it. She became a mother's little helper and Leia was glad of it. She was able to get an extra nap in because Landon wasn't sleeping through the night, not yet anyway. This required energy to stay awake during the day. But by the end of the third week she was feeling almost back to normal. She felt good.

Keri took her and the baby to the doctor. She discussed with her when she could do things such as driving, exercise and working a little. She told her to keep moving but get plenty of rest and eat right, also drink fluids, juices, milk, etc. if she was continuing with the breastfeeding. She would pump her breasts so that others could give her a bottle when she went to the restaurant to help out. She liked the idea of others helping, so she wouldn't feel overloaded by doing everything herself.

By the middle of October, Leia was in a groove with the baby, his sleeping patterns, helping the family she lived with, and three lunches a week in town. Tracy surprised the family with a vacation. He told them at dinner one night. He'd received seven free nights at a timeshare near the Grand Canyon.

"Who wants to go to the Grand Canyon next month?" he asked his family at the dinner table. Everyone agreed, a yes in unison. "Leia and Landon, too. I'm renting a van which seats eight, so there's room for the car seat. Babies sleep a lot anyway," he said.

A few of them laughed and agreed. All of a sudden there was so much chatter about what they would do at the Grand Canyon.

Chapter Fifteen

Seven hundred miles or so would be covered, in this journey to one of the Seven Wonders of the World. Keri checked out a book on the Grand Canyon for each of her children, appropriate in age. Tracey left at midnight so that most of the driving was done while the children were asleep. It would be difficult for him but he'd have his wife drive later, and he'd take a nap. Better this than restless and bored children fussing in the van or worse yet, endless voices uttering 'I have to go to the bathroom.'

He headed south to Colorado and would go there by way of Albuquerque. They would stop by for an hour to visit some family. He looked back in his rearview mirror and everyone was asleep. Right behind him was Leia and next to her the baby named Landon. He couldn't see him as he was in a car seat facing the back. All the children in the way back could see the baby. Aspen was behind Keri and the other three: Autumn, Montana and Tallulah were in the last row. Behind them were supplies, such as a cooler and food in boxes. He had put the luggage up top in a carrier.

Tracey stopped at a drive-thru to get some coffee and surprisingly, no one woke up. He got back on the highway, and turned on the radio, lightly, to keep him company. He sipped his coffee and looked down the highway and off to the horizons and city lights. He felt lucky with how the ranch had worked out for him. It had been three long years of hard work but he had managed to make it work and become a business. He felt bad for Leia, but was glad now she was living with them. That old house would most likely be condemned soon, and probably, be burnt. He knew that was coming.

He'd checked the weather and anything could happen this time of year. It could snow or be a warm 'Indian Summer' as the Americans liked to call it. He'd prepared Keri to pack accordingly.

When they arrived it was the latter, a warm Indian summer. He'd been given a three-bedroom condo for a week not too far from the canyon. They unpacked the car and tomorrow they'd hit the trail.

Landon was sleeping through the night so that was good. She and he had a bedroom to herself, but since it had a double bed Aspen asked if she could share her room and Leia readily obliged.

Keri made sandwiches for everyone in the morning before they departed; she packed some snacks and drinks, too. Yesterday afternoon she'd made a trip to the store to supply the condo for when they would come back. She couldn't wait to see the canyon.

Autumn brought her book of facts about the Grand Canyon, and began to give out these facts to everyone in the van.

"Listen to this, the Grand Canyon was carved out by the Colorado River in Arizona. It is one of the Seven Wonders of the World," she stated.

"What's a wonder?" asked Montana.

Leia answered this after Tallulah spouted out, "I'm a wonder, Montana!"

Autumn continued with the length being 277 miles long, 18 miles wide and an unbelievable, mile deep. A few of the kids looked at her with this fact. "That's what it says," she said convincingly.

"It's possibly 17 million years old and some people, named the Pueblos, thought it to be a holy site." Autumn explained how the Grand Canyon had some of the cleanest air in the United States and that it had big horn ewes, coyote, skunks, raccoons and bobcats.

"I know what a bobcat is. I've seen one before," Montana said.

"Where have you seen a bobcat?" asked Autumn.

"I don't remember," she added. "Maybe on television."

"Well, it looks like a cat but bigger. The head is much bigger, but it is fairly harmless. Some people have had them as pets."

"Okay, this lesson is over because I see the Grand Canyon!" she shouted and pointed.

Everyone looked in her direction, and off to the right one could see far off in the distance a ridge. Sure enough it must be the Grand Canyon. Forty-five minutes later it was before them.

The curtain was lifted. The land so colorful it painted a color by number in so many hues. Words were not spoken but beauty was seen, unlike anything they'd ever witnessed. Keri got her camera ready and Leia had a baby carrier, a knapsack type frontal carrier she would place baby Landon in.

Out of the van and in front of them was a site so spectacular; one wondered if your feet were firmly planted on the ground. They walked over to the ledge and along the pathways to view. Grand it was beyond any scope. Leia only wished her baby could see all this. She had Tracey take a picture of both of them on his cellphone. She would look at it later.

The group toured the Bright Angel Lodge, which was made of stone and logs back in 1935, by a lady designer. Autumn informed them. It was very old and they looked in the gift shop and the sitting area, where people back in the olden days had tea.

The group found a picnic area, and Keri brought out the sandwiches, drinks and snacks. After lunch, they would take a walking tour which would last about three hours, and then return to the condo.

The next day they had planned another tour, farther down the way and more remote.

When they woke up the next morning, it had snowed a couple inches, and the kids couldn't resist running outside to touch all the white flakes. Maybe, they wouldn't drive as far today, and save it until tomorrow. For sure, though, they had to go and see the Grand Canyon in all its white glory.

String the Cranberries

Chapter Sixteen

The family spent the week at the Grand Canyon, coming and going, never tiring of staring at the beautiful site. One day Leia purchased some stationery, and decided to write Brandon, not sure of when she would mail it, or where to send it but she felt he needed to know about them.

Out near the canyon the weather felt very warm that day, and the family had all gathered nearby. She sat at a picnic table, and wrote him a letter. She looked over at the Grand Canyon, and the splendor of it all. A couple times she peeked over at Landon laying in his car seat and smiled. Leia was happy, very happy at this moment. What was it?

Looking at the Grand Canyon made her dilemma seem like it didn't exist. She felt moved, lighter, and ready for what may come. At this moment she felt empowered, like she was in control. She made a plan. What did her mother ask of her? She remembered she'd asked her to tell Brandon about the baby before Christmas.

Christmas was two months away. She must find a way to go and see him. First, she must find him. She felt ready. She guessed she needed this time for her and the baby to be situated, to know each other, to feel comfortable and strong. Just in case he decided he didn't want to be in their lives, she'd be strong enough to handle that. Now she knew she cared (about him) but it wouldn't destroy her. She smiled and looked up again. Yeah, the Pueblos knew a good thing when they saw it.

One of the days, Tracey and Keri, decided to take a helicopter tour.

This one didn't go over the canyon but along the edge. They asked Leia if she wanted to go, but she declined. She did want to see the beauty but she had a little life that depended upon her so her decision came quickly. She'd watch the crew with Aspen's help, and she sent the two of them on the trip all by themselves.

Leia tucked the letter away and thought she'd look into his whereabouts right after Thanksgiving. For now, she was having a wonderful time at the Grand Canyon. She found it very easy to travel with Landon; he was portable and easy. He was also becoming more alert, looking all around, and cooing was the newest thing he did. It was adorable, and the kids just loved it.

Later on Tracey and Keri described the helicopter trip as exhilarating and awesome, like nothing they'd ever done in their lives. The pilot talked to them and showed them spots along the ridge and explained the whole history and how it developed. The pilot said their service stopped going over the canyon after several deaths occurred, but he assured them the trip they took was just as spectacular, without the danger of wind currents.

On the ride home everyone seemed to be in a great mood, playing with some of their trinkets, cards and games they'd purchased. All agreed the Grand Canyon rocked.

Chapter Seventeen

*L*eia continued her weekly schedule. She worked in town at the Painted Pony several lunches a week, and helped at the ranch with the horses and barn work the other days. Then she assisted with meals during the week, and looked after Landon the rest of the time. She enjoyed reading with the kids at night and some of them read to Landon. It was as though he had a big extended family with four big sisters. He was the only boy child in the house, so the girls found this amusing. He received loads of attention.

Marissa and she became friends working at lunch in town. The kids were gone to school during the day, so this gave her two days with the baby alone. Keri watched Landon while she worked at the bar, and was always there to help her if she had any questions. Tracey was a big support, too. One night after dinner she asked him if he had an address or phone number for Brandon, if he knew of his relatives. He said he'd look at his books to see. He knew his last name was no help as it was Smith. These days he said it was pretty easy to find someone, but he may have moved or be living with someone else. She told him she wanted to go and see him before Christmas. He said he'd let her know what he could find out.

Leia opened a savings account in town at the bank, and banked every dollar she could. She knew it was important to do this. She knew she couldn't live forever at the ranch. She tried not to think about this, but it crept in, and so, she diligently put aside most of her paycheck and the dress money. Her food and immediate needs for herself, and the baby were provided for in exchange for helping Keri at the ranch.

She felt lucky.

What if she were still at that old haunted house she and her mother inhabited? The painting had only given it a lift as it decayed further under the false covering.

Thanksgiving was here and she helped Keri and the whole house prepare a turkey. It was snowing outside and parades were on television, and children were running around everywhere. They were going to put the tree up tomorrow, and Keri asked her if she was going to be around.

"Are you going to town or shopping on Friday?" Keri asked her.

"No, no plans of shopping," Leia responded. "I do have to work the lunch time, though."

"Oh, okay. We'll miss you with the tree, but we'll save the garland, cranberries and tinsel for tomorrow night. Sound good?"

"That would be great," she said and smiled. She went and gave her a big hug. "Thank you so much. You have done so much for me. You have saved my life with all your help."

Thanksgiving Day was festive and full of fun. The two families had bonded and would probably, forever remember this precious time they helped each other out. Tracey had told Leia he couldn't find where Brandon had gone, he never had a phone, and the only other name was an uncle named Sam. He was a barber and so he was looking into that.

He'd let her know when he found Sam.

Friday at the Painted Pony was fairly lively as many customers came in after being house bound from the day before. Also, customers who were shopping in town for Christmas or Holiday gifts were having lunch. She waited on a couple of locals she remembered from school. They were hands on another ranch, out towards the opposite side of town. They were being very friendly, and one of them seemed interested, especially in talking with her. When he came up to pay the bill he seemed a little nervous but she smiled at him. Then he asked her out, and this took her by surprise.

She'd been asked out on a date.

Well, that had been a long time. She thought about it, and she really shouldn't say no, she needed friends. She guessed she might need a boyfriend. He seemed nice enough, and so, she said yes.

He took her to the movies the next day, Saturday, and she enjoyed it. She thanked him, and she actually did have a good time.

Chapter Eighteen

Tallulah came running up to Leia when she saw her, "Leia, see the sign?"

"Sign? What sign?" she asked her.

Tallulah pointed to the front window. She looked at her, and pointed again.

Tracey heard her, and knew what the fuss was all about. "Tallulah is pointing to the new ranch sign out by the road."

"New sign?" she questioned again.

"Leia, they put up the sign for the ranch. I finally got around to putting up our family name. I had one made. I'm going to put the old one up back here on the barn," he said.

"What does it say, Tallulah?" she asked the three year old.

"Jackson," she cried out.

"Jackson, that's your last name," Leia said. The little girl smiled back at her. "I can't wait to see it. Does it have anything on it?"

"Buffalo on it," she replied.

"Buffalo, that's cool. Is there anything else?" Leia asked.

"Numbers, too," she told her.

"I put the year we started here on it. 'Jackson Family Ranch established 2000.'"

"Great! I'll be looking for it," Leia stated.

"Leia, I need to tell you something else. The old house is going to be burnt down next Saturday, so you may want to go and retrieve anything else you might have missed when you moved out. I can send one of the ranch hands to help you. Just let me know when," Tracey said.

"Okay, yes I should do that, although there can't be much left. I sold most of the furniture and some went to the bunkhouse."

I'll give you some boxes you can pack the personal items which you may want to keep."

"Sounds good. I'll do that on Friday."

Friday morning came and it was cold out and snowing, but she had a job to do, so her and Jesus went to the old house, and began the process of sorting through items. She hadn't been there since a few days after the funeral when some people bought a few of the larger items, namely furniture. She'd moved hers to the ranch house, and sent a few pieces to the bunkhouse like the kitchen table and unused dressers.

Now she had to go through more kitchen items and her mother's bedroom, including her personal belongings. She should have done this already but hadn't gotten to it. She'd been pretty busy. Jesus dropped her off to give her a few hours to herself, and said he'd come back. He asked if that was okay, and she said yes. She would be all right.

Climbing out of the truck brought back memories of her and her mother in the backyard, this was all too fresh but the baby had kept her very busy. Jesus put the boxes inside the kitchen door, and said he'd see her later.

She looked around the semi-deserted kitchen, and recalled some good memories. She and her mother had every meal together here for three years. Her aunt had spent plenty of time in this house, almost every Saturday. Leia wasn't a great cook but her mom had taught her the basics. It seemed like Landon had replaced her previous life.

She packed up what was left in the cupboards, which wasn't much. Probably the ranch hands could use a few more dishes. She had nowhere to put these so she would give it all away. When that was done she took a few paper towels, and began to wipe the counter. Why was she even doing this? *Because this is what she used to do,* she thought.

Back in the corner was an old glass vase with some Queen Anne's lace, probably from the roadway, though, she didn't remember ever picking any and putting it in the vase.

Maybe her aunt had been here after the funeral. There was some mail underneath the glass, and Leia picked it up and sorted through it. She remembered the day her mom died she had gone to get the mail, and had never opened it. Since that time Keri or Tracey had picked up her mail, and brought it to her. She or someone must have put it way back in the corner, and she missed it when she took her things to move into the ranch.

She leafed through the envelopes and most of it was junk mail. One was a letter with an Illinois return address. She eyed it curiously, and saw Brandon's name on it. What?

Quickly, she opened it. She wanted to sit down, so she turned and jumped upon the counter. The light from the kitchen window allowed her to see, and read the words written by her friend she hadn't seen now since last December. She wondered why after all this time he was writing to her.

Dear Leia,

I'm writing again to let you know how I'm doing. I hope you are well. I miss you.

What have you been doing all this time? And how is your mother? I hope it isn't too hard on you lifting her, and doing it all by yourself. She's a very nice lady. I miss the ranch. I learned so much, and wish I could have stayed longer. I miss you, too. Did I say that?

It's been snowing and snowing and snowing. The land is a white blanket and it's very cold. I bet you have snow, too. Christmas is coming soon, and I miss you. I wish I could see you this year. I can't believe it's been a whole year. Did the little ones from the ranch make you a pepper wreath this year?

You never wrote back, and so I don't want to bother you much. I thought I would give it one last time, and then I won't contact you anymore. I had hoped my letters would have found you feeling the same. Do you feel the same? I hope so.

I miss you,

Brandon

Tears flooded her eyes, and streamed down her face. She was consumed, and overwhelmed. She was confused. What letters? She looked around; she had never received any letters from Brandon. Not one. She read the letter again.

She went looking around, opening up drawers, and looking for any sign of unopened mail. She ran to her mother's room, and went scavenging through drawers and then the closet and even the pockets of old clothes. What was she doing, certainly her mother would have given a letter to her. Wouldn't she?

Again, she became confused. She never had his address, but he had hers because he had been here before. They must be somewhere and how many were there?

She stopped for a moment to think. If her mother did get a letter then she must have hid it where she could reach or place it. She went to her bedside stand and got down on her knees, looking and probing. Sure enough she found an envelope with a letter.

What did her mom say to her, "Promise me you will go, and see Brandon, and let him know about you and the baby? Promise me Leia."

She had promised her. She read the other letter, and became stunned.

In it he told her why he had to leave so suddenly, and that she should come and visit him. He asked if she had read the letter he left at the Painted Pony.

No she hadn't seen a letter nor did anyone give her a letter. She became somewhat frenzied and knew what she had to do. She had to pack up what she wanted here, and load the boxes into the truck when Jesus returned. Then they would go to the Painted Pony in town. Marissa might know something, or where to find another letter.

She did a once over after packing things up. She didn't know why her mother never gave her the letter; she was upset over this, but just couldn't understand it. Maybe she didn't want her to leave and leave her all alone.

245

Chapter Nineteen

"Jesus, can you go faster?" she asked him. She was anxious, and wanted to make this trip quick, as she needed to get home to the baby. Later tonight she could sort through all of this, and decide what to do, and when to do anything.

"Leia, I'm going the speed limit. Don't worry, we'll get there and we will be in one piece," he added.

He was right she needed to settle down, as it had been a year. There probably wasn't any letter, after all this time. The place had been shut down and reopened when a new owner bought the place. Certainly the place had been cleaned out or something.

"I know, I know you're right," she said and looked out the window. It was December. She needed to think about what she needed to do before Christmas came. Brandon came by train; she probably needed to go by train if she was going to visit him. She didn't even know what a train trip might cost.

She bundled her coat closer to her body, and grabbed her purse as she exited the truck. Leia practically ran into the Painted Pony. She looked around for Marissa, and once she found her she hurried to her side.

"Can I talk with you, do you have a minute?" she asked quickly.

"Sure. What's up?" Marissa asked with concern.

Leia took a deep breath, and tried to calm herself. How could she phrase this and get right to the point.

"Marissa, I think Brandon may have written me a letter, which I never received. I'm thinking it might still be here, somewhere in the bar. He said he left it in the bar, last year," Leia said.

Marissa looked at her and tried to remember the last time she saw Brandon. "The last time I saw Brandon was last Christmas," she said.

"He left New Year's Day, kind of in a hurry. He didn't say goodbye but told Jesus he had to go back home. No one has heard from him," she said.

"Leia, you of all people should know that is not unusual when it comes to ranch hands or help on a ranch. People come and go, all the time."

"I do know that, really I do. But Brandon and I were getting close, very close. I want to go and see him and tell him about Landon. It's a long story but I just found a letter from him and in it he said he had written a letter and left it here."

Marissa thought some more. He was writing a card to someone the last time she saw him.

"He did write out a card the last time I saw him. I thought it was for Tracey, and he was saying goodbye," Marissa explained.

"Did he put it anywhere, or did he go and mail it?" Leia asked.

"The place was sold and we didn't reopen for months," she replied.

"Let's go back to the office and check back there."

The two ladies went to the office but found nothing there. They began to look behind the bar on all the shelves. Under the cash register was a cabinet; it contained old accounting books from the previous owner. Marissa could see the dates and started to look for last year and January of this year.

"Here's one, let's look at this," Marissa said.

When she opened it up, a letter fell out from the pages. Leia quickly grabbed it and read the handwriting. She had it. She couldn't believe it. She looked at Marissa with big doe eyes. Unbelievably, she felt relieved.

Marissa quickly looked for any other letters in the book. There was none. Someone must have put it in here from the mail pile the day he wrote it, or when the owner had a heart attack and then it sat in here all this time. She shook her head.

"You gonna be okay?" she asked her coworker.

"Yes. Yes, I am now," she exclaimed. "I'm going to read this at home. Thank you so much. Thank you."

"Leia, you are welcome. I'm so sorry it was hidden in here," she said, and waved goodbye to her friend.

Leia didn't wait until she was at the ranch. She opened the letter immediately after she climbed in the truck. Jesus started the engine, and turned the radio on. He looked over at her and seemed pleased. Too bad Brandon didn't tell him about a letter or rather give it to him, then, this could have been avoided. He was guessing Leia missed him, and it was very important to her to know what he had to say or why he went away.

Jesus got a call from Tracey and answered it as he was driving. "Oh okay, thanks. Yeah, we're on our way back, now."

"You okay? He asked Leia.

She looked over at him and then went back to reading her letter, words from Brandon that seemed to light the page on fire. That's what it seemed like. She missed him; she realized it very much now.

When she finished she looked up, and she held the money in her hands. He had left her a letter and money to travel and visit him, when she could get time away from her mother. She thought she was going to cry, and when she looked over at Jesus she almost did.

He had to tell her and he was unsure how she would react.

"Leia, they are setting fire to the old house."

"Yes, I know," she replied.

"I um mean they are doing it now. Just so you know," Jesus said.

A couple minutes later they drove past the burning fire in the middle of the field of grass. The fires flames' reached high, and were bright orange; there was no wind today. She could see flames reaching out the windows after more oxygen eager to make ashes of the homestead. Tears fell from her eyes for the second time today. She gasped for breath and was in need of a glass of water to quench her sudden dry throat.

The whole day was too much for her. She collapsed when she went to exit the truck and Jesus went around to her side. He picked her up with the letter in her hand and carried her inside. He then set her down on a sofa where she quickly came to. Keri came over to see what was happening and then sent Jesus to get a cool rag, even though it was winter outside.

Jesus explained to her all the excitement and emotional upsets she had just received. Keri shook her head, and told him she'd handle it if he needed to go. He quietly left knowing Ms. Keri would take very good care of Leia.

When Leia became more aware, she handed the letter to Keri to read the address on the outside. Her look of surprise became one of astonishment when she looked at the date.

"How could this be?"

Three days later Tracey took Leia and baby Landon to the train station. She insisted she would be fine traveling to Chicago with Landon. She was unable to talk with Brandon as he had moved but Tracey had contacted Sam, Brandon's uncle, at the barbershop. She told him the story but asked him to not tell Brandon. Leia wanted to see him and talk with him herself. He understood and said he would pick her up at the train station. Sam did relate to Tracey that Brandon had spoken of Leia, quite often actually, and missed her.

Leia packed her winter clothes, then Keri gave her a very warm coat for her and the baby. Landon was four months old and actually quite easy to travel with. He slept peacefully in his car carrier and he was taking bottles. She had packed dry formula for the train ride and several toys to keep him occupied. He liked his little fuzzy books and could turn the pages all by himself.

Tracey put them in his truck and drove Leia and Landon to the train station. He felt responsible for her; she had lost so much in her young life. Yet, here she was with a baby, and going to see the father. What would happen? He didn't know. But the uncle named Sam, seemed to think this was a good idea. He genuinely thought this was the right thing to do. He looked forward to meeting her and taking her to see Brandon. He would keep it a surprise.

It was cold out here in Wyoming and probably colder in Chicago. She'd seen the TV reports and Chicago had as much snow, if not more. Leia wore knee length boots, not cowboy, but styled with a warm knit navy blue dress underneath a long camel double-breasted dress coat. Keri had given her this special outfit.

Landon had a baby onesie under a legless wrap and a hat to boot. She had a blanket for extra protection just in case they had to be outside for any length of time. In addition to her purse she carried a backpack full of diapers, wipes, toys and a change of clothes for any accidents which babies were known to have.

She hugged Tracey and said goodbye. She added, "Thank you for everything. You and Keri have been so kind and have done so much for Landon and me. I am not sure I can ever repay you."

"You're welcome from both of us. We'd do it all over again. We'll see you soon. You two have a good trip," he said.

"Thanks," she said. She paused and added, "Merry Christmas!"

"Merry Christmas, Leia," he said, and waved goodbye as she walked away.

She boarded the train and found her seat. She placed the car carrier in the seat next to her, and looked out the window. This would be her first trip ever by herself.

She looked over at Landon; he was awake and looking at her. *What was he thinking,* she wondered?

Once the train began to move, he was lulled to sleep from the motion and quiet persistent noise. That was good. She'd probably give him a bottle after a little baby food jar. Leia smiled and closed her own eyes. The journey was set in motion, no turning back. She was only going forward with hope in her heart, based upon the letters she'd finally seen after almost a year.

He didn't even know about this little being who sat next to her. She hoped he might just fall in love with this miracle like she had. She fell into a light sleep, always listening out for Landon, just in case he awoke before her.

How she fell asleep, all hopeful and full of bright anticipation is not how she awoke. What if he was with someone else by now? She hadn't even thought of that. What if he was married? Her eyes grew big and worried.

She looked around and saw a couple with two kids ahead of her. Then she looked over at a lady with her husband, both elderly and Leia thought she scowled at her. Her expression was not warm. She looked down. She had no wedding ring on and she was traveling alone. This was not the dark ages, but for a minute, she felt judged. She felt not right when others were married. Then she remembered her mother's words, please go and tell him before Christmas, let him know. She became comforted by her mother's words, even if she was dead. She carried her with her in her heart and mind. Mother's know these things; *they are wise,* she thought.

She fed baby Landon and before giving him the bottle she made her way to the bathroom. A little change of scenery would be good for him. He needed to be out of the carrier for a while. She laid him on the bathroom floor while she attended to herself. The train was only half full, she surmised. This left plenty of room to walk about and look out the windows.

A lady said hello, and asked her some questions. Then she said, "Have a seat here for a few minutes. It's empty."

Why not, she thought?

The woman was probably older than her mother and seemed interested in chatting. They talked about and to Landon. He reached out to her trying to touch her hair. She touched his cheeks a little and seemed very preoccupied with making him smile, which he did a lot. For some reason Leia told her everything and most of all the reason for this trip she was taking.

The woman blessed Leia, and said that was one of the best things she could ever do, was to tell the father. He should know she told her. He is a part of his life whether he has an active part or silent part. Raising children, she told her is a very difficult job, and it's always a good idea to have help, even a little bit of help.

This conversation is what Leia needed to hear, someone with her mother's ideals and full of good advice from living a life. Wisdom.

Whether it worked out, she didn't know, but it's good that you try. And if it doesn't work out, then you will have done everything you could. That is what she took away from sitting next to this soft-spoken older lady.

An angel right here on the train her mother might have said to her. She liked to say that when someone appeared out of the blue, and gave you nothing but kindness. People like that exist, her mother would say, just when you least expect it. Leia could definitely use a dose of that, and it came just when she least expected it. She smiled at her and excused herself. She told her it was time for a bottle and an afternoon nap.

$$Chapter\ Twenty$$

eia arrived in Chicago late that night close to midnight. She departed the train and looked around for Sam, Brandon's uncle. Tracey had given her a description and said he'd meet her there when she stepped off the train. She didn't have to look very long for he came right up to her, and offered his hand to carry the car carrier.

"You must be Leia, correct?" he asked.

"Yes I am, and this is Landon," she said, and let him take the car carrier.

"I can tell as you are the only one here with a baby," he said, and smiled broadly.

"Let's go. We can talk in the car. I'm sure it was a long day on the train."

"Yes, it was. Thank you so much for meeting me," she uttered. She shivered. It was cold, especially at night. It was bitter cold and the wind didn't help at all.

She followed him out of the station and out to his car. He seemed like a nice guy.

He helped her into the car after he placed the baby in the back seat. Landon was sound asleep. The car warmed up quickly, and he began talking quietly, and telling her how long the trip to his home would be. He had a room for her and the baby could sleep in there, too. His wife had pulled out a bassinet she had from one of their grandbabies. Actually, it had a fancy name he couldn't remember. It was one of those portables.

"A pack-n-play. I've heard of those for people that travel or need another bed in another room," she said.

"Yeah, that's it. It will work perfectly for you. You can use it as long as you are here, okay?" he said.

She looked outside and there were so many buildings and homes, everywhere. They kept going from street to street through stoplights and over highways. They arrived at what appeared to be houses connected to one another with front porches. One had to go upstairs to reach these doors. He parked in front of one and stopped. Here we are. This is home.

His wife came out to greet them. She helped Leia with her bag, and let her take the baby.

She told her to follow her and come right up. They went through the front door into a warm and lovely place, filled with inviting furniture all neat and clean. She followed his wife, named Beverly, who showed her to her room so she could get the baby settled. Come out to the kitchen for a few minutes after he goes asleep. I've made something for you.

She did what was asked and met her in the kitchen soon after Landon went down for the night. Beverly had made her a sandwich and offered her a couple Christmas cookies, which she had frosted earlier.

"What kind of cookies are these? They are so good," Leia said.

"You like those? Those are gingerbread. You've never had those before?" she inquired.

"No. No, I haven't. The ones we used to make are white, sugar cookies, and we frost and decorate them, too."

"These have molasses in them. These are my favorite. I'm glad you like them. You can have more tomorrow," she said, and smiled.

"Sleep in or as long as you can with the baby. There is a washroom down the hall if you need to freshen up or take a bath or shower. Sam will be gone very early to the barbershop. We'll go out to see Brandon tomorrow night, all three of us. I mean all four of us, oaky?" She instructed Leia.

"Thank you. Sounds good. I must go to bed now," Leia said.

"Good night and nice to meet you," Beverly said quietly.

Today was the 19th of December, Beverly, Sam, Leia and Landon spent the morning in the couples' family room. Beverly turned the Christmas tree lights on and baby Landon seemed mesmerized by the lights. Beverly suggested they go down to the local store and do a little shopping. Maybe they should take a few presents with them when they went to go see Brandon.

Neither Beverly nor Sam had said too much about Brandon except that he lived outside of town. It would take a couple hours to get there and they would spend the night and return the next day. Leia said she would like to do some Christmas shopping, which was a good idea.

Beverly bought quite a few items, mostly clothes in different sizes, children's clothes. She told Leia she had several nieces and one nephew she needed to buy presents for and then wrap when they got home. Leia bought a couple things for Landon and also a shirt for Brandon. She felt funny buying him something but would rather have something than not when they arrived at his home. She also bought a candle for Sam and Beverly, for their home and some candy, too.

While baby Brandon slept in the late afternoon, the two women wrapped the gifts they'd purchased and listened to Christmas music via the stereo. Leia found herself humming some familiar tunes, and she enjoyed this company with this woman she'd met only last night. They were being so kind to her and Landon. Beverly doted upon little Landon and Leia.

Around 5:30 pm Sam arrived home with a to-go dinner he'd bought on the way home. He set the burgers and fries on the kitchen table, "Just as you ordered my lady, fast food!"

Quickly, they ate and readied themselves for the trip. Arrival would be just at dusk, Sam estimated.

Leia looked out the window as she sat in the back seat next to Landon. Everywhere she looked she viewed snow. It lay on the ground and several feet of it. They drove on an isolated highway through farm acreage with an occasional house and barn and a rare large tree, which may have provided farm animals' shade from the sun in summertime.

There wasn't a farm animal to be seen, it was as though the beautiful white blanket stopped the world and said take notice. This is the time for you to be with family, Christmastime, and inside with a fire, a tree, some music and cookies. Her anticipation was mounting and she couldn't help but smile. Beverly looked back at her and smiled, her eyes full of happiness. It wouldn't be much longer.

Sam slowed down and made a couple turns off the divided highway.

Leia had been occupying Landon, to keep him from crying or maybe wanting to get out of the car seat, when she looked to see that Sam had turned into a driveway.

It was a long driveway, but not nearly as long as the ranch in Wyoming. Large bushes lined one side of the drive and several large trees were leafless in the front yard. Right out front bushes circled the front of the home and a gate closed the opening, which then began a paved entryway to the front door. *How pretty* thought Leia. She gazed upon this glorious winter wonderland.

Snow lay in blankets on all the bushes, trees and yard. It was still coming down. She could see lights on inside through the windows. It was not quite dark. Sam parked in the drive, and pulled right up to the attached garage. It wasn't big but it was *quaint and elegant* she thought.

This was it. The time had come. She hoped she didn't frighten Brandon with her and Landon. *What a surprise* she thought. But everyone had been so nice to her. And she was willing to walk away and leave him alone.

She had promised her own mother, she would do this and let him know. Doomsday briefly flooded her mind, and then she picked Landon up from the car seat. She stood tall holding her little bundle.

Sam left the packages in the trunk while Leia left the car seat; Beverly said they'd come back out later to get the gifts and such. Beverly rang the doorbell, and the guests could hear the scurry inside. A girl with long reddish-blonde hair answered the door with a couple others right behind her.

"Hi," was all she said.

"Hello, Adele. Remember us?" Sam asked.

"Yes. It's uncle Sam!" she yelled into the hallway.

"Merry Christmas," cheered Beverly.

"Let them in," someone hollered from the kitchen.

She let them in opening the door wide. The family dog came around sniffing and jumping up a little on everyone.

Sam shut the door behind them as Brandon came into the hallway. He said hello to Beverly and Sam, and then looked upon Leia with surprise.

Sam jumped in with, "Brandon, you remember Leia?"

Brandon could hardly believe his eyes, in fact he didn't. He didn't know what to say, and so he walked right over to Leia and smiled brightly.

"Leia."

"Brandon."

"Leia, this is the best surprise, ever. I've missed you," Brandon said eloquently.

"I've missed you, too," she replied sweetly.

"Please, come in folks. We are busy in the kitchen. Come back and join us."

The travelers walked in, and made their way to the kitchen. Christmas music was playing, and the kids were all gathered around the kitchen table. The littlest one was wrapped in her mother's arms as she gave her a bottle. The woman, named Riley, sat in a wheelchair, and looked up at the visitors.

"Welcome. I'm so glad you both came and you brought us special visitors, I see," said Riley.

"Yes, this is Leia. She's Brandon's friend from Cheyenne, Wyoming," said Beverly.

Leia beamed and held up Landon to face the family. She looked at Brandon and said, "And this is Landon, my son. He was born in August."

Brandon stood there silent and looked at Leia in a quiet moment.

Leia looked back and smiled, then nodded ever so silently a stilled yes with her head.

He walked over to Leia and put his arms out to hold the baby. She gave him to Brandon with pride and joy in her heart.

Riley missed nothing of this exchange, and called for Cierra to come and get Cheyenne from her arms. After she was relieved of him she spoke to Leia. "What a beautiful baby and very young. You've come a long way to see Brandon and traveled by yourself."

"Yes, I did. I'm so glad to be here, to see Brandon again," Leia said, not sure what else to say at the moment.

"I know he's glad to see you. He's talked about you. I feel like I know you. He has said wonderful things about you. He thought he would never see you again and here you are," Riley said.

"Thank you. You are so kind," Leia said.

Sam saw the table and asked, "What are you making? It looks like you are sewing."

Chloe, the five year old, replied jubilantly, "We are strunging the crayberries."

"She means stringing the cranberries!" Adele corrected her matter-of-factly.

Leia with a soft voice repeated, "Stringing the cranberries, how wonderful."

"They are making garland for the Christmas tree, something Brandon brought back from Wyoming. Ever so often somebody sticks themselves, as hard as they try not to," Riley added.

Brandon announced that it was bath and pajama time. All the kids followed his direction, and left, even Alex, who was three. He handed Landon back to Leia and said he needed to help and then picked up Cheyenne. He followed the kids upstairs to help holding the littlest one.

Riley picked up things around the kitchen, maneuvering in her chair fairly well. Leia took note of this, after all, she'd cared for her mother for years.

Sam and Leia went out to the car to retrieve the packages and portable crib he'd brought. Beverly and Riley cleaned up and settled out in the family room around the tree.

Beverly held onto Landon and sat upon the couch. He would be in need of a bottle soon and diaper change. Maybe she'd send Leia and him upstairs with the rest. She decided to do that.

Later the two came down after baths, and books read. Everyone was down, for now anyway. Brandon expected none of them would get up tonight as they had played in the snow most of the day. It was sure to tire them all out.

"Would you like to go walk in the snow?" he asked her.

"Yes, that would be nice," she said.

The rest of the adults talked a while and prepared for bed.

Chapter Twenty One

The couple walked outside through the snow, the flakes had stopped coming down and the air was clean and brisk. She told him about her mother's death last summer and he stopped to hold her and comfort her.

"I'm so sorry, I wish I could have been there for you. You were pregnant at the time, did you have the baby early?" he asked. Both were preparing for the inevitable words to come.

"Brandon, it was hard, so difficult. She made me promise her something," she said.

"What was that?" he asked in earnest.

She looked at him and tried to read his eyes. "She made me promise her I would tell you about the baby. Landon is your baby. You are the father. But you knew that, right?"

"Leia, when you walked through the door and I saw you holding … Landon. I knew then. Sam said nothing, but that he had a nice surprise for me. What a surprise," he said.

He leaned over and kissed her forehead, and then wrapped his arms around her.

She sighed heavily.

They continued walking and went around back near the barn. He let them inside where it was warmer. Once inside he took her face into his hands, and looked deep within her eyes.

"Your mother was a lovely lady who looked out for you as you took care of her. She loved you so much. She gave you wonderful advice, and I am thankful for that."

He kissed her softly and then kissed her for a year's worth of missed kisses. She responded in kind and with utmost respect and devotion. He said what he had longed to say, since he left her last January, "I love you, Leia."

"I love you too, Brandon," she said.

"Now let's hear what happened to my letters, and why you waited so long," he said.

On the way back to the house she explained everything, which she had discovered about what happened.

"I thought about calling, in fact, I told Riley that was on my New Year's resolution list. I was going to call the ranch, and wait for someone to answer. You know after the letters I sent, I did call twice but hung up. I'm not sure what I was scared about. I just didn't want to interfere in your life with your mother, and really with the five kids I barely had any time.

He went on to explain the tragedy that occurred and his reason for leaving so fast. Once he got home, Riley was in a coma for a few days but she survived the car accident whereas her husband had not. Josh died immediately and Riley had a long road. There was no other family, only Sam. "He called me home," Brandon told Leia. "I had to come home when he called, as he had done everything for me since my parents died."

"I became this instant father of five. Riley became wheelchair bound and you know what that is like," he said.

"Yes. Yes, I do," she said.

"I knew you would understand. I did the best I could and then when Christmas came this year, I made a decision. I would do this but I needed to see you and call you. I was going to invite you one more time to come here. I hoped you would but knowing my dilemma and your mother, I didn't see a way this might work," he explained.

"I do understand completely. Oh I do," she said in kind. "You made a New Year's resolution, too."

They kissed lightly one more time and then came back into the dark house. He showed her to her room and said good night. He was so pleased. He couldn't wait to see her in the morning. "We have a son!" he said and smiled.

"Yes, we have a son," she said.

A few days passed, Sam and Beverly stayed an extra day and then went home. Leia stayed with Brandon for the time being and the house was full.

On the night before Christmas the house, full of love, gathered around the tree, strung with cranberry strings made by little and big hands, and sang a couple songs. Then they left cookies out for Santa and a glass of milk. Riley read a Christmas story and then all went to bed.

Christmas morning was terrific. Brandon assisted Santa and managed to get the presents wrapped. With Leia's help they dispersed them around the tree before morning. Chaos ensued once everyone was awake. Later that day Brandon had a special treat lined up. The neighbor down the road was coming by with his horse and sleigh to give everyone a ride over the white landscape.

This was the highlight of the day, and kids laughed and were merry, and oh, so bright. At the end Brandon and Leia went for a ride by themselves. He showed her the countryside and explained that he had saved money out west and in addition to his sister's land and house he'd purchased the property right next door. Though, he hadn't done anything with it yet.

He showed her where he could put a house on the land and a barn, too. He had learned so much out in Wyoming, he hoped to maybe farm and keep some animals. He would build it slow. She reminded him that she knew a lot about animals. He remembered that, too.

"We best get back and work on the dinner plans. Kids got to eat you know, like all the time!" he said loudly.

"Like babies do!" she remarked.

When they came back to the front of the house, the kids were building a snowman. They thanked the neighbor for the ride and helped the kids to build a couple snowmen. Adele went inside to get a couple carrots for noses and some extra hats. Alex found some rocks for buttons. Brandon wasn't sure where he got them from as the ground was completely covered.

Riley had made hot chocolate for all, and served it up when they came inside. She told them she wanted to go outside later when they went sledding. She wanted to see their happy faces going down the hill outback. It wasn't a very big hill but big enough.

She sat out back and watched her brood go down the hill, over and over, with laughs and smiles, and a good amount of time expending all their extra energy.

Leia and Brandon even went down a few times. It was fun! It began to get dark and Brandon made a fire outside so they could all roast some marshmallows on a stick.

Leia was dressed warmly with a hat and mittens and had Landon all dressed up, you could hardly see his face. She had an extra blanket just in case the wind picked up.

The group sang some songs around this campfire, outside on their farm in Illinois. Leia was so proud of Brandon and all he had done for his sister. She couldn't believe the love she saw on the kids' faces and their mothers' face. She knew they must miss their dad, but today, and tonight, on Christmas night there was joy and thankfulness. Brandon was a part of this family with all his help and love and care he gave to them.

Christmas night, a night for all the nights filled with love and family. That night her and Brandon tucked everyone in to bed, no need for a story as when their heads hit the pillows, sleep ensued quickly.

He helped his sister to bed, and made sure she was okay. He knew she missed Josh but he wanted to assure her he would be there for her, even with this new little being who suddenly came into his life.

"Landon is beautiful Brandon. I don't want to interfere with your future life," she said.

"Riley, you are part of my life and these kids. Remember, I bought all the land next to you," he assured her.

"I know, you do so many things for me. I could never have kept all the kids with me, if not for you. I am forever indebted to you," she said.

"We are sister and brother. We have each other as there are no others. I will always take care of you. Maybe someday you will meet someone again, and then I will still help. I will always be close to these kids and now they have a cousin," he added.

"A cousin," she said.

"I'm going to ask Leia to stay here, that's if she wants to."

"That is a good idea. I think she does like it here," said Riley.

He pulled the blankets up over his sister to cover and tuck her in, "Thank you for being such a wonderful sister and mother. You are a good person."

"Thank you Brandon."

"You're welcome!"

"Good night, Brandon. She's a very lucky gal to have you."

"And I her. Good night sister."

The End

9 781988 680071